Ton T

The Colour of Death

The Colour of Death

A Sebastian Foxley Medieval Mystery
Book 6

Copyright © 2018 Toni Mount
ISBN-13: 978-84-948539-1-3

M

MadeGlobal Publishing

For more information on
MadeGlobal Publishing, visit
our website
www.madeglobal.com

Dedication

For Glenn: technical advisor, social media liaison, financial manager, valuable critic, chauffeur, coffee-maker and best friend who just happens to be my husband. How lucky am I! I couldn't do it without him.

Why not visit
Sebastian Foxley's web page
to discover more about his
life and times?
www.SebastianFoxley.com

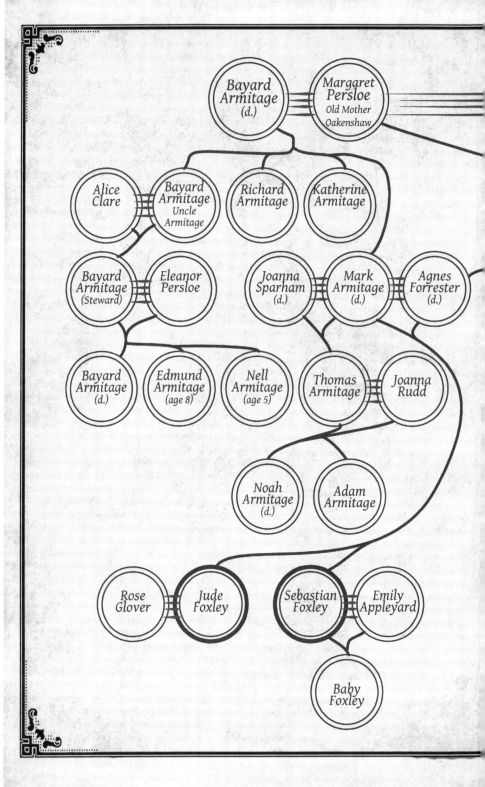

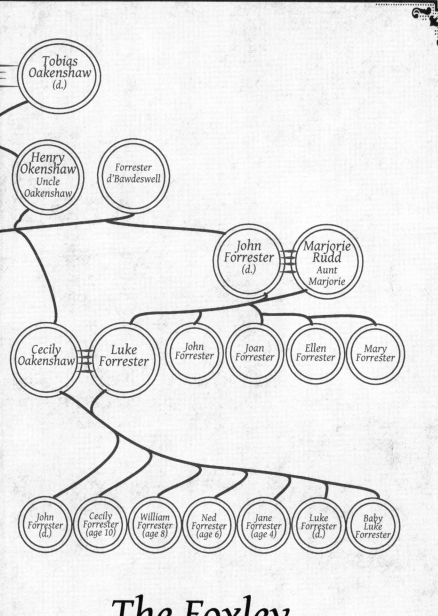

Tobias Oakenshaw (d.)

Henry Okenshaw Uncle Oakenshaw

Forrester d'Bawdeswell

John Forrester (d.)

Marjorie Rudd Aunt Marjorie

Cecily Oakenshaw

Luke Forrester

John Forrester

Joan Forrester

Ellen Forrester

Mary Forrester

John Forrester (d.)

Cecily Forrester (age 10)

William Forrester (age 8)

Ned Forrester (age 6)

Jane Forrester (age 4)

Luke Forrester (d.)

Baby Luke Forrester

The Foxley Family Tree

Prologue

THE CHURCH of St Thomas was small, modest by any measurement but adequate for the village. It had but one feature that made it exceptional: the painting of the Last Judgement, a huge mural that filled the space betwixt two large windows in the north wall of the nave. It had been there for centuries, gradually fading into the plaster, the occasional vivid contrast of a smear of vermilion or azurite showing where it had been retouched in the past to prevent it disappearing forever. It wouldn't do to let the parishioners forget what fate might lie in store for them: heavenly bliss or, more likely, the eternal agonies of hell.

One lone figure stood to the right hand of the mural, as stark and awful as the day it was first painted: Death, in his guise as the Grim Reaper. The pigment used must have been made with candle-soot and had not faded down the years as the rest of the image had. A more terrible forbidding likeness was hard to imagine, skeletal hands gripping his scythe, hooded and cloaked in black: the colour of death. It sent shivers down the man's spine just to gaze upon it. That was as it should be.

He liked to take a few moments to admire the painting and was intrigued by the work of the in-comer from London. Despite his odd way with words, the visitor claimed to have been born in the village, although the man had no memory of him as a child. Whatever the case, the fellow said he was a limner, skilful with paints and pigments, and he'd offered to repaint the Judgement for no charge upon the parish. Of course, both Father John Haughton, the priest at St Thomas's, and the parishioners had been eager to accept such generosity, but the man was suspicious: no one did anything these days for

1

no reward. Perhaps the limner – a skinny fellow calling himself Sebastian – expected to receive recompense in the next life, in which case, the man reckoned, he'd be disappointed.

Mind you, he did have some talent. Already, a radiant Christ in Glory was seated upon a gorgeous rainbow. The pigments were bright as might be wished and the Saviour's face was that of a living, breathing man. This, he disapproved. The figure had an expression far too compassionate, as if He might overlook all but the worst of sins and such humanity was quite wrong for God sitting in Judgement upon the Day of Wrath. Clearly, the limner's vision of that terrible day was mistaken.

Watching the way this Sebastian fellow climbed the ladder so cautiously, as a man wanting a second pair of hands just to hold fast, wobbling along the scaffold boards all unbalanced, the man doubted that the mural would ever be finished. Most likely, the drunken limner would fall and meet the Grim Reaper long before completing the task. The man's gaze returned, as though summoned, to the fearful hooded figure. Thinking of Death – a subject that had been much upon his mind of late – the man recalled his fellows, outside in the churchyard, about to cut the hayfield on the manor land across the way. Just like the Reaper, they too were armed with scythes: innocent workmen's tools and he thought how easily they might be transformed into implements of execution.

And one individual – particularly offensive to every upright Christian man – deserved to be removed, before he corrupted other souls. As any decent goodwife would sweep such foulness from her doorstep, so he would cleanse the village. But not for him a broom; rather a well-honed scythe blade would do the task and make good the Grim Reaper's reluctance: too slow in performing his grisly office. The man was determined to have the manor of Foxley a wholesome place once more.

He turned away, leaving the limner alone at his work once more, stepping out into the benevolent sunshine of a fine June day.

Chapter 1

Monday, the fifteenth day of June
in the year of Our Lord 1478

At Foxley, a village in the county of Norfolk

I LOVE THIS village – the place of my birth but otherwise quite unknown to me 'til these last few months. I lived all my life in London but now feel this small manor to be my true home. When first we came, I found the wide expanse of sky strangely intimidating. In London, everything was enclosed by the works of man, whether houses, workshops, churches, warehouses and, of course, the mighty edifice of St Paul's Cathedral. But here, you can see the horizon across the flatlands, broken only by the trees of Foxley Wood. I could bear such open space because I told myself I thus had a better view of Heaven; that here was a vast cathedral created by God's own hand with mighty oaks and elms for pillars and the sky itself for a roof.

It aided me that I have family here, too: cousins aplenty and even an elder half-brother, Thomas, from my father's first marriage, of which I knew not. The only relative I recall my father ever mentioned was a sister of his, though whether older or younger than himself I did not know, nor even her name. I now know she was somewhat younger than he and named Katherine, that she wed a cloth merchant of Norwich and went to live in that city. My Aunt Marjorie who told me this says she has heard naught of Katherine for some few years and knows no more of her. It seems unlikely then that I shall ever meet her.

As for myself, I am growing used to being known as Sebastian, the son of Mark Armitage, instead of Seb Foxley as I be called in London. I would be content to stay here always if I did not, eventually, have to resume my former life in the city to earn my living. The generous purse of Lord Richard, the Duke of Gloucester, my patron, will not last us indefinitely.

Unfortunately, though I be happy, the same cannot be said of Emily, my dear wife. Em has little liking for so much sky and says she misses her friends, despite the best efforts of my new-found family to make her feel most welcome. Aunt Marjorie Forester – the widow of my mother's brother – has done everything in her power to put Em at her ease, as have my maiden cousins, Joan, Ellen and Mary Forester, and the wife of Cousin Luke, Mistress Cecily, though with five young children, she has little time to spare to help Em feel at home. There is an uncle and a cousin also on my father's side, both named Bayard Armitage. My cousin has done well for himself as both the Steward and Bailiff of the Manor, holding his offices from Edmund Grey, the Earl of Kent and Lord of Foxley. Since the earl comes but rarely to the manor, Uncle Bayard – forgive me: Steward Bayard – holds sway over the law here.

I have also come to hold dear Old Mother Oakenshaw, my father's mother, though her name be different as she married Tobias Oakenshaw after my grandfather's death. There is also a half-uncle to me from that marriage, Harry Oakenshaw, he who runs the Nether End Tavern and is father to Luke's wife, Cecily. These relations confused me mightily at first, but there is one I have become especially close to. In truth, he be my half-nephew, son of my much older half-brother, Thomas, but we be of an age, Adam Armitage and me. He even took an apprenticeship as a scrivener and book-binder to a stationer in

Norwich – a family tradition, it seems – so we have much in common to speak about. Adam's father, Thomas, had already married and left home when our father, Mark, wed his second wife, Agnes, who bore Jude and me. I try explaining this to Emily, but she throws up her hands in despair and says she'll never unravel the tangled skein that is the Armitage family which makes me Adam's uncle when he be my elder by a month or so. I tell her it matters not and to think of him rather as a dear friend of mine instead.

Afore we came here, having to flee London for safety's sake when the Woodvilles were intent upon slaying me, Father John Haughton and Aunt Marjorie persuaded Steward Bayard to make available an empty cottage for Emily and me. By the time we arrived last March, upon the twenty-first day, on Holy Saturday, our new home stood ready for us. This done by the generosity of folk who, despite some being my relatives, were utterly unknown to us, yet they welcomed us to their village as long-lost cousins. The cottage was in good order though it had been empty nigh a twelvemonth since the death of the last tenant – a frail old man distantly related to Aunt Marjorie, such that she had some vague claim upon the tenancy to be made good by her nephew: me. As Lord Grey's tenant, I owe him a week's labour at haymaking and harvest but, in honesty, I shall not make good the terms. Sebastian Foxley has never gripped a scythe in his life and would probably hack off his own feet at the ankle, if ever he tried. Instead, in exchange that others will do my share of work in the fields, I have promised to repaint the wonderful mural in their church at no cost, to save it from fading away. This is work I can do.

'What will you be doing today?' Emily enquired after we broke our fast on bread and ewe's milk cheese.

I was grinding red lead and yellow ochre pigments: a great deal of both.

'I shall be painting Hell's mouth. Can you not tell by my choice of colours?'

Emily nodded.

'You will take care up on that scaffolding, won't you? It looked more precarious than ever at mass yesterday. I don't want you hurt.'

'Fear not, Em. I shall be cautious. But what of you this day? If you take those eggs to Old Mother Oakenshaw, tell her I'll visit as soon as I may and mend that leaky window for her. It requires a new sheet of oiled parchment.'

'Oh, I don't know, Seb. I'm not much in the mood for trailing over there today.'

I watched as my wife prised herself off her stool and began stacking our platters. She was great with child and ungainly, tiring easily of late. She put the treenware ready to be washed and pressed her hands to the small of her back.

'Do not overtax yourself, sweetheart,' I told her. 'I don't want to return to find you lugging buckets from the stream, as I did yesterday. That task can await my return at dinnertime when I shall fetch water, if we need more. Promise me?'

Em nodded, but I was unconvinced.

'Swear it,' I said.

'I swear.' She sighed heavily and eased down upon the stool. 'Don't be late. I have a rabbit ready to stew. Your cousin Luke brought it for us yesterday, fresh caught, which was a kindness indeed, although I think he had no right to it, so the sooner it's eaten, the better. Your family seem to think naught of breaking the forest law, poaching game.'

'That would appear to be the way of it here,' I said with a shrug. 'And he is the lord's forester by his craft, not only by name. Just enjoy the bounty, Em, build your strength for the coming babe.' With my ground pigments securely stored in my scrip, I kissed her upon the cheek and left to walk to the church, followed as always by my faithful dog, Gawain. He was grown to quite a size in the three months I had owned him. No longer a ball of black and white fluff that I could tuck inside my jerkin, he was long-legged now with large paws and could ever outpace me. But he knew me well enough, that I was no runner, and though he bounded ahead, he would always wait for me to catch up before going on again.

I made my way up The Street – one of Foxley's only three roads that branched off the highway betwixt Bishop's Lynn and Norwich, the others being Manor Lane and Mill Lane. For the rest, there were only footpaths. On my left hand as I began the gradual ascent – as close a thing to a hill in these flat Brecklands – was Nether End Tavern. Our Tavern, as it was called. At the far end of The Street was Upper Tavern, also known as the Grey Arms. This latter was a larger and, so its customers claimed – the Meades, Butts, Persloes and the rest – a far superior drinking establishment compared to Nether End. We disagreed as a matter of course. Nether End ale, brewed by Harry Oakenshaw, was better and stronger, as testified by its greater number of drunken Armitages, Foresters, Rudds and Parfitts on a Saturday eve. Rivalry was fierce and the tug-o'-war and archery competitions betwixt the two alehouses, planned for the forthcoming St John's Day revels, were likely to be contested with much enthusiasm. It was likely the Nether End would win because we had that giant among men: Cousin Luke.

The sun was already warm upon my neck; bees hummed contentedly in the dust-dappled grasses at the roadside and the snowy stars of stitchwort sprinkled the verge. But a few weeks since, bluebells had spread a royal tapestry here. Now the dainty yellow of Our Lady's bedstraw and the purple sentinels of knapweed replaced them. I paused to listen to a linnet's melody and waved to Aunt Marjorie and Cousin Ellen, busy draping their washing along the quickthorn hedge. It would dry swiftly and bleach well on such a beautiful June day. Not only linen adorned the hedge. Wild roses blossomed in profusion and honeysuckle scented the air. Meadowsweet set its creamy spires in every damp patch along the way and I thought I must gather some upon my return, for Em: some to strew on the floor at home and some to brew her excellent headache remedy.

The lichen-shadowed stones of the church of St Thomas the Apostle rose from the sheep-cropped grass of God's acre; its bell tower the tallest building for miles around. I took the great key from its box in the porch to open the ancient door. For such a large key – sixteen inches long by my estimation – the keyhole had also to be of such a size and, so the tale ran, large enough that a wren had once built her nest in there. Fluttering out as the key was inserted, she gave the priest such a shock, his heart nigh failed him but, being so kindly, he ordered the door remain unlocked until the wren's fledgelings were flown. Such was the story, at least.

Inside, the church was cooler than the summer sunshine outside. Gawain followed me through the door, knowing the procedure by now, and found his usual place behind the font to snooze away the morn. Such is a dog's life though I knew, at the least excuse, he would be up and chasing anything from dust motes in a sunbeam to Old Mother Oakenshaw's ferocious gander, if he dared. But I had trained him to mind his manners within the church.

'God be with you, Seb!' Adam Armitage called out, entering the church as I was about to climb the ladder up to the scaffolding. 'Be you in need of assistance up there?'

'God give you good day, Adam. You could pass me the other pots of pigment, if 'tis no trouble? How is your mother faring this morn?'

'Oh, crabby and crotchety, as ever. I swear she takes the greatest pleasure in complaining and today it be that the sun will prove too hot later and wither her crop of peas on the bines. Whereas yesterday, she was bewailing the lack of sunshine was stunting their growth.' Adam handed me the pots of ochre and red lead that I had ground earlier, having to climb the first few rungs of the ladder in order to reach, despite being a tall fellow, like my brother Jude. It was a trait that ran on both sides of my family:

the Armitages and the Foresters, so I had discovered. But Cousin Luke Forester outstripped all the rest in height and breadth. I had never seen the like except for the Duke of Gloucester's friend, Sir Robert Percy. Luke made dwarves of the rest of us.

'Be careful on those boards. I wouldn't want you coming to grief, Seb, you know that,' Adam added. 'You mean so much to me.'

'Fear not, Adam. Once I get up here, I be safe enough. 'Tis just the ladder that troubles me.'

'Well enough then. I'll be away to the manor; see what lists Uncle Bayard would have me draw up this day. No doubt but he'll have a mountain of papers for me to deal with. Endless scribbling is all it is.'

'You sound like my brother Jude.' I sat on the boards, level with the faintly visible fires blazing within Hell's mouth that gaped horribly on the right-hand side of the mural. I loaded my brush with red lead pigment. 'Will you come and share dinner with us later? Em has promised a rabbit stew.'

'I shall be there, Seb, Uncle Bayard permitting.' Then Adam was gone, leaving only Gawain to give me company in the quiet church. Yet I sang a *Jubilate Deo,* "Be joyful in the Lord", as I painted for the sheer pleasure of creating a work to the glory of God my Maker.

I thought about Adam as I laid on the layers of pigments. We had grown dear to each other in just a few months. Most likely, it was because we each saw a likeness in the other to our absent brother. It surprised me, how much I missed Jude back in London, running our business, hopefully. By now, he should be a married man, if his wedding to the lovely Rose had come to pass, as intended. I had missed that also, sadly. But Adam's loss was greater yet. Not a twelvemonth since, last harvest-tide, his twin brother, Noah, had been gathered to God. He and Adam were devoted and much alike in appearance but quite dissimilar in temperament: Adam was the village clown, keeping folk laughing with his merry jests. Noah was the quiet, serious, thoughtful one – like me, as Adam kept insisting.

The tragedy had begun with a bramble scratch on Noah's wrist. It grew inflamed and did not heal. Noah became feverish and the wound festered. Days passed and he grew worse. In desperation, Adam had walked – or run – the nigh unto twenty miles to Norwich to fetch a surgeon, praying he would return in time to save his brother. He was gone for five days by the time he had persuaded a surgeon to come and they walked back to Foxley. Noah was still alive, but his strength was ebbing. The surgeon informed the family there was little to be done; the arm was beyond saving, but the young man might live, if the now blackened limb was amputated right swiftly. The task was soon done, but Noah died in Adam's arms within the hour.

Adam blamed himself. Either he had been wrong to hasten and fetch the surgeon, wasting those precious days when he could have sat with Noah, giving him the strength to recover, or else he had been too tardy in bringing the surgeon, leaving it too late to save his brother's life. No one could convince Adam that he was not at fault and the laughter in the village – Adam's merriment – died also upon that day of sorrow. He even admitted to me, in confidence, that so bereft was he that he had gone to that same bramble patch and deliberately gouged his arm on the thorns, determined to join Noah in the grave. Yet his wound had mended quickly and cleanly with scarcely a mark to show for it.

When Em and I arrived in Foxley, back in the springtime, Adam's grief was yet raw but, upon an instant, he concluded that I was the answer to his prayers: his beloved brother returned to life. Of course, I was no such God-sent consolation, but Adam insisted that I must be. Was I not an Armitage of the same age and temperament? It must be so and he refused to have it said otherwise. Besides, since he reminded me somewhat of Jude, we became close companions, almost brothers, and he was content. The village was a merrier place once more as Adam's spirits revived and that was all my doing, so Aunt Marjorie told everyone. It was pleasing to know I served a purpose.

The mural too was reviving. The fires of Hell leapt to life beneath the strokes of my brush. Another few days, by my reckoning, should see it finished. I heard Gawain stir and make a noise of greeting. I washed out the brush in clean water and looked down. A stocky man of middle years stared back at me, a deep frown of disapproval drew his greying brows together above his prominent nose. He leaned heavily upon a stick – his unwarranted reminder of the battle of Towton, fought far to the north some years ago. It was a savage, blood-soaked contest, fought in a snowstorm, as he never tired of telling anyone who would listen, in which he had heroically saved King Edward with his own hand. So he said, though few believed his tale.

'God give you good day, Uncle Oakenshaw,' I called out. 'No customers in your tavern at present?'

'Nor ought there be at this time of day. They're all at their labours – as should you be.'

'I am at my labours, uncle. This is my work,' I said, raising my hand towards the mural.

'Call that work! You're idle, you. Get a hoe and pruning hook in your hand. Do some proper work, as God requires.'

'I am serving God to the best of my abilities in the ways I know how. I know naught of fieldwork, ploughing and pruning. Forgive me, uncle, I must get on with this afore the pigment dries out. I'll not disturb your prayers.'

'You'd better not.'

Uncle Harry Oakenshaw was a testy fellow indeed, but no one could fault either his sincere piety or his skills at brewing ale, so his dour humour was overlooked by the customers to his tavern. He came to pray, alone, every morn.

I returned to my painting, enjoying the magic of fresh colour enlivening the faded image of fire. The original underlying plaster had a roughness to it that gave an element of texture not found when working on parchment. I made use of this, highlighting some few of the most prominent grains in the plaster with white lead pigment, seeming to create enlivening sparks amid the flames. I was pleased with this effect.

The sun shining through the south windows and a rumbling belly told me dinnertime was not far off. I dare not be late and my pigment pots were empty, so I rinsed the brushes and set them to dry, tip uppermost in a pot. Taking the greatest care – as others had warned me – I clambered down the ladder. Fortunately, the warmth of summer had driven out the worst of the stiffness in my hip and such activity was easier for me than it would have been in the winter's chill.

On my way down The Street with Gawain running before and singing as I strolled, I paused to gather a bunch of wild roses, meadowsweet and other hedgerow flowers for Em, certain they would cheer her. Gawain, impatient of my dallying, bounded ahead. He set up an excited commotion, his husky bark occasionally reverting to a puppy's yap – just as a lad's voice might break – and I saw Adam awaiting us. The dog greeted him with a thrashing of his tail and a thorough washing with his tongue. Adam accepted such joyful treatment with steadfast patience, standing in the shadow cast by an old oak tree, its trunk so gnarled and strangely contorted, it was said to be as ancient as the church, from before the time of William who called himself the Conqueror. Mayhap, it was true.

'Down, Gawain!' I commanded, more than surprised when the creature obeyed my order and came trotting back to my side. 'So, Adam, did Steward Bayard have a mountain of papers for you to deal with, as you feared?' I asked him as we walked on towards our cottage that lay at the lower end of the way, by the turning into Manor Lane.

He clapped a hand on my shoulder and laughed.

'Not so much, God be praised, and of those there were, most were fit for fire-lighting. Why he needs to note and account for how many grooms and stable lads forget to make use of the barber's services each quarter, I cannot think. We all of us grow beards, except you. Why is that, Seb? Be you not yet of age, little lad, to grow one?'

'Beards be unfashionable in London and I have taken up the habit of putting a blade to my chin at least twice each week.'

'Ah, fashion, is it? I suppose the king shaves so everybody else does likewise, is that it? The women too?' He laughed and so did I. 'But not your comely Emily, of course.'

''Tis a fact, Adam, that women of discernment in the city do shave off their eyebrows.'

'To what purpose? Your Em doesn't do that, does she?'

'No, not Em. As to the purpose, I have no idea.'

'They'll be shaving their armpits next and who can say where else. I'll wager the barbers will eagerly pay for that privilege and every last fellow will be clamouring to serve the apprenticeship.'

'You be a rogue, Adam. Only you could think of such a thing.' I raised a hand to acknowledge Nicholas Parfitt who hailed us as he strolled with Meg Rudd, his light-o'-love, towards the Nether End Tavern, where she worked for Uncle Harry Oakenshaw.

As we came in sight of the cottage, set a little back from the way, hidden by a hazel coppice, we saw quite a gaggle of women at the door. Friends and neighbours stood around, chattering like excited magpies.

'What's the to-do, Cousin Mary?' I asked Aunt Marjorie's youngest daughter who sat on the doorstep, juggling some old pine cones.

'You can't go in, Cousin Seb, nor you, Cousin Adam. Mam says so.' She moved suddenly to catch a cone gone astray.

'Why not? 'Tis dinnertime and I promised Em I would not be late. Cousin Adam is joining us.'

'Well, he cannot and there'll be no dinner for either of you. Mam says you can go to our house and eat there with Luke and the children.'

'Why?'

Mary sighed, as if I was a fool to require an explanation.

'Because Em is busy.'

'With what task?'

'Come away, Seb. This be no place for us menfolk.' Adam pulled me from the door. 'Let's go eat with Luke, as instructed. You don't want to be here. Trust me.'

'Not until someone tells me what be amiss.'

'Lord bless us. Can you truly be so unknowing?' Adam said. 'Shall I borrow your brushes and paint a picture for you? Em's travail must have begun. The babe is coming, Seb.'

'What? No. That cannot be.'

'Why not? Do you expect her to carry that burden in her belly indefinitely? It has to come out sometime, else she'll burst.'

'But she would have said this morning, if 'tis to happen this day. Would she not?'

'Perhaps she didn't realise.'

'How could that be?'

'Don't ask me, Seb, I've never given birth.' Adam leaned back, puffed out his cheeks and thrust his lean belly forward, waddling all ungainly. 'You may as well ask those cows over there; at least they've calved not long since.'

'But I ought to be with Em. She'll need me there.'

'No, she won't. Women do childbirth their own way and they don't want men getting under their feet. Your Aunt Marjorie wouldn't let you, anyhow. Come. I'm hungry. Let's see what's for dinner at your aunt's house.'

'You be certain, Adam?' I asked, leaving my offering of flowers by the door.

'Lord's sake, Seb. Sit down and eat your dinner, can't you? You be digging a gutter in the floor with your to-ing and fro-ing.' Adam was enjoying his meal, but I could not think about food. All my concern was for Em.

Adam and I had joined the Foresters for dinner, at least those who were not attending Em, which meant my cousins, Luke and John, and Luke's little ones.

'Leave him be, Adam,' Cousin Luke said, dishing out my share of food into their bowls. ''Tis his first child, isn't it? I recall I paced all night long when Cecily birthed our eldest, even out in the pouring rain. Isn't that right, John?' he asked his younger brother who nodded as he ate. 'And I wasn't much better when Will came along, either. Mind you, by the time we'd had Ned, Jane and Little Luke popped out all of a rush, I was past caring. Now she tells me there's another stirring in her belly, I think I'll move to Norwich.'

'You'll just have to keep your breeches fastened, Luke. How many children do you own to now?'

'Five, as you well know, Adam.'

'And the rest, spread across three parishes? We all know there are more by their build. You can't deny them, Luke.'

'Well. Is it my fault God blessed me with the bollocks of a bull?' Luke grinned.

'No woman is safe with you around, even the ugly ones. And what do you say, Seb?' Adam grabbed my jerkin to keep me still. 'Eh? You think Luke could abstain for a year or two?'

'Sorry. What were you saying? I must go home. 'Tis taking so long. Something untoward must have happened,' I said as Adam shoved an ale cup in my hand.

'Cease worrying, cousin,' Luke told me. 'Babes sometimes take days to arrive.'

'Days! Dear God,' I squawked, crossing myself.

'It's been barely above an hour or two since the womenfolk went dashing off to your cottage.'

I drank the ale without realising.

'How did they know to go? Did Em come to ask aid?'

'I was in the forest, at my work, with John, clearing the rides for the earl's hunting party at the end of summer. Young Cis, do you know?' Luke asked his ten-year-old daughter.

'Aunt Joan was passing in the lane, I think... or was it Aunt Ellen? Whoever it was saw Emily doubled over by the stream,' she said.

'I told her not to go, carrying buckets of water. I told her. Now she be injured.' I was so frantic, I made to rush out the door and go to Em.

Luke pulled me back and there was no way I might oppose his strength of arm.

'The pangs of childbirth, is all it is, cousin. Have some more ale.'

And so it came about, the three of them – Adam, Luke and John – plied me with strong ale all afternoon and, by eventide, I was more drunk than a Bankside doxy. The first time ever. And the way I felt next morn, it would needs be the last.

Chapter 2

Tuesday, the sixteenth day of June

'YOU ARE a disgrace, Sebastian. Look at you! Whilst your lovely wife was suffering her travails to bring your child into the world, the best you could think to do was drink yourself into oblivion. I am ashamed of you.'

Aunt Marjorie was correct to chastise me so but, in truth, her shame was naught compared to what I felt. And that was only a small part of my grave discomfiture, all in all: I was so ill, I was certain I was about to knock upon Death's door. I had awoken before dawn and that was early indeed at midsummer. I had crawled outside the Foresters' cottage to throw up my bellyful of ale and lain out on the roadside until the sun was well risen. Its terrible glare had pierced my eyelids and entered my brain like red-hot iron nails, such that I dragged myself back within the shade of the thatched roof. That was where my aunt had found me when she returned from the cottage where Em and I dwelt. Luke, John and Adam were all snoring on the straw pallets spread upon the floor, but she had stumbled over me, curled by the wall outside with only Gawain to keep me company. He alone demonstrated no disappointment nor censure at my pitiful condition.

'How is Em?' I managed to ask, forcing the words off a tongue so furred and vile it felt as if uncured goatskin lined my mouth.

'Ah, so you can finally turn your thoughts to where they should be.' Aunt's wrath was barely abating. 'She is exhausted but in good heart. A strong lass, your Em, and matters went well, God be praised. You have a fine son, nephew. Not that you did anything to deserve such a blessing.'

'Well done, Seb,' Adam said, grinning like a gargoyle.

'Well done?' my aunt queried. 'What has he done to deserve your congratulation, eh?'

'I'll go to her...' I began to say.

'No you won't, not yet and certainly not like that. See the state of you! You're disgusting in those clothes. Get that jerkin and shirt off.'

I hesitated.

'Come along,' she urged. 'I've seen enough naked men in my time and your unclothed body will revolt me less than those puke stains.'

Reluctantly, I obeyed. Only as I bundled them up, did I realise how much my garments stank.

'And your breeches: they're no better. Luke, shift yourself and find some of your father's things for your cousin to wear.' She crossed herself at the mention of her late husband. 'They'll be a nearer fit than any of yours. And I blame you for this, my lad. I would lay money – if I had any – that you were the one refilling his cup every time. That's the truth, is it not, Luke Forester? You're a bad influence on us all.'

'Aye, Mam: right as always.' Luke sounded chastened, but the glint in his eye said otherwise. He stretched and yawned before ambling over to the family's linen chest and throwing back the lid. An assortment of clothing was soon piled in an untidy heap on the floor.

'Have a care! Those things are clean and *were* neatly folded.'

By this time, Luke's wife, Cecily, had returned from our cottage and began rousing the children. She looked weary indeed as she knelt by the hearth to rekindle the fire, ready for cooking. But then all the womenfolk must have been working throughout the night and I wondered when Em's babe had made its – his – appearance.

I stood there, in the midst of the floor, wearing naught but my nether clouts, attempting to cover myself. I felt humiliated, but no one was giving me a second glance. I realised how different things were when the whole family dwelt in one room with but an extra small space beneath the eaves, gained by climbing up a ladder, where the four older children and Cousin Mary slept. Luke, his wife and babe, my aunt, Cousin John and my other two unwed maiden cousins, Joan and Ellen, all slept down below, by the hearth. It was not like London here in the sticks.

At last, my aunt had restored order to the linen chest and chosen some garments for me. 'Tis true, they were smaller than anything Cousins Luke or John might wear but they were still over large on my lean frame, though the breeches were of a fair length. The shirt hung off my shoulders, so the sleeves covered my hands and I rolled them up. The jerkin was likewise far too broad, but I used my leather girdle-belt to pull it close and to prevent the breeches from falling about my ankles. I might be cleaner and smell better, but I must look like a scruffy street urchin in my borrowed clothes. At least I was no longer naked.

Aunt nodded approval.

'You'll suffice, I dare say. But make sure you stop by the stream and wash the puke off your face and out of your hair before you go home.'

I scrubbed at my cheek and could feel the skin stiff with dried vomit. I was so ashamed, yet my aunt smiled at me.

'Be of good cheer, nephew. We all make mistakes and do things we regret after. Now go to your goodwife and meet that splendid little son of yours. You're a father now, with new responsibilities. Remember that.'

'I will, aunt. And thank you for caring for my Emily... and the babe.' I smiled at the thought that Em had come through her ordeal. And now I had a son! I was unsure how I felt about that. Fatherhood was a grave weight of responsibility. What if I was unsuited to the task? Supposing I was found lacking and failed in my duties? It was a sobering prospect; one I did not feel prepared to face.

Our cottage seemed spacious after the crowded home of the Foresters as Gawain padded in before me. Cousin Joan was tending the fire and baking unleavened bread on the hot hearthstones – something Em had learned to do since we came here. Cousin Mary was on a stool beside our bed, singing softly to what appeared to be a bundle of linen lying in her lap. I supposed that was my son. The dog went to her, to sniff at the new smells but was, instinctively gentle, as if he knew. I saw that Emily was sleeping soundly.

Refreshed by a thorough wash in the stream, my hair yet damp and my headache much improved, I tiptoed over to the bed.

'She's asleep,' Mary said, unnecessarily. 'She's tired out. You want to see him?' She held out the bundle towards me.

I panicked and backed away in haste. I knew not how to hold a babe and the very thought was terrifying.

'Er, no. You both seem quite comfortable there. I shall not disturb you.'

'You're scared, Cousin Seb.' Mary giggled. 'Why are men always afeared of something so small? So foolish, aren't you?'

'Don't mock, Mary,' Cousin Joan told her. 'It comes natural to women but not so to men.' Joan left the bread and came to take the babe from her younger sister. 'Sit on the stool, Seb, and I'll put the mite in your arms. You'll soon get used to it.'

I did as I was told and Joan settled the well-wrapped parcel in my lap. It weighed so lightly that I wondered if there was a babe within at all. She turned back some of the linen, revealing a tiny blotched face with plump cheeks and pursed lips. Aunt Marjorie had called him 'splendid', but I could not have described this strange little creature so. It made a faint mewing sound and I wanted to give it back, but both women were now busy, preparing food. It yawned, showing a moist tongue and toothless gums, before settling again. What was I supposed to do with it? I dare not move for fear of disturbing or dropping this fragile thing.

'I see you're getting to know our son.'

I had not realised Em was awake. Seeing her, I wanted to embrace her, kiss her, but the babe was in my lap.

'Are you pleased?' she asked. 'He's so beautiful, isn't he?'

'Aye, well, aye. Of course I am pleased. He's, er, in truth, Em, I cannot see much of him in all this swaddling.'

'Pass him to me. He'll be needful of a clean tail-clout. You can see him without his bindings then.'

Awkwardly, I managed to give the babe to Em without dropping him. My wife laid the bundle on the bed, across her lap, and began removing pins and unwinding the swaddling bands. I watched in awe, wondering how she knew what had to be done. Seeming to read my thoughts, she said:

''Tis a good thing Bella Langton showed me how to do this when Janey was very small. Now, see?' Em lifted away the tiniest open-fronted shirt to reveal skin as pale and velvety as the petals of the roses I had gathered in the hedgerow, yesterday. 'Count his fingers and toes: ten of each. Is it not a miraculous thing, Seb? He's so perfectly made.'

I was about to agree when she removed the tail-clout. That a body so innocent could produce something so foul...

'What's amiss with it, Em? It must be sick or something,' I said, retreating swiftly.

'No. 'Tis always like this the first few times, your aunt told me. Apparently, it improves in a day or two. Put the clout over in that tub to soak, will you?'

I hesitated so long that Mary snatched it away and dealt with the offending linen, tutting loudly as she did so.

'Come, break your fast, Cousin Seb,' Joan called. 'The bread is fresh baked and the bacon collops crisped at the edges.'

What with an ale-sick belly from last eve and the sight of that tail-clout, the very mention of food proved too much for me. I fled the cottage, tripping on Gawain and colliding with Adam beyond the door as I hastened behind a convenient bush to retch and heave, unseen. My privacy was short-lived. Adam came to me.

'Still poorly?'

'Let me be,' I moaned. 'I want no company.'

'I came to see the babe; not to give you sympathy. It's your own fault.'

'You and Luke were the ones all but pouring ale down my throat.'

'How were we to know you can't hold your drink? 'Tis not us at fault. You should have warned us.'

'I did not know either. I have never been drunk afore.'

'Never? I thought everyone in London got pickled as herrings.'

'Well, they don't. And I swear I shall never do so again.'

'I've heard that oath enough times, Seb, to know it's soon broken.'

'I make an oath; I keep it.'

'For certain you do,' Adam said, but he winked and laughed.

'I mean it.'

'Aye. So do they all, until tomorrow. I've sworn that same oath myself too many times. Now, are you going to show me your new son and boast about his legion virtues as a father ought, or not?'

I straightened my borrowed clothes and breathed deeply.

'I don't know about legion virtues, Adam. In truth, I know not what to make of him at all but, I suppose, I shall get used to him.'

'You don't have much choice in the matter, do you?'

'No. I fear not.'

'What have you called him?'

'He's a babe.'

'Aye, but he still needs a name. You'll be having him baptised tomorrow, won't you?'

'Oh. I hadn't thought so far. I suppose I must speak with Father John to arrange it.'

'Then he'll be wanting a name... and godparents. Have you decided who they will be yet? As an upstanding and blameless parishioner, I willingly offer my services. Then you may call him Adam to honour me.'

'Two Adams in this small village? One like you be more than sufficient, I think.'

'I feared you might say that, but the offer stands, whatever name you give him.'

'Godparenting is a serious task, Adam; a deal of responsibility. Back home, I am godfather to a little maid: Janey Langton, though I fear I be failing in my duties at present, for obvious reasons. In the same way, how would you perform your duties when Em and I go back to London?'

Adam shrugged.

'The same will be the case whoever you choose, won't it? Better me, who's unwed and free to travel, if ever I please, than someone whose livelihood is here in Foxley. I could live and work anywhere. If ever there was a need, I could come to London.'

'I hadn't thought of that.'

'Truth is, Seb, you don't think beyond drawing your next breath,' he said with a laugh which somewhat removed the sting from his words. Nevertheless, he was correct. Ever since we arrived in the village, I had not dared consider the future. I lived each day as it came, thankful for every new dawn that saw me still living, despite those who had tried to kill me in London. Now I would have to look ahead. For my son's sake, if naught else.

'Come see him, then. I hope Em will have him decently clad by now.'

'Unlike his father.' Adam flicked at the endless loose folds of my borrowed shirt. 'And watch you don't drop those breeches. God knows, a whole family might live in them besides you. If you don't have a spare pair of your own, I could lend you my Sunday best, so long as you promise not to wear them for painting.'

'I do have others. I just hadn't got around to changing into them.'

We stepped over the threshold, out of the bright day, back into the secluded gloom that was the newborn's first sight of the world. I wondered how much my son's eyes could see of it, or were babes born blind as puppies?

'God give you good day, Emily.' Adam said, 'And may I be the first man to offer you my heartfelt congratulations on your motherhood.'

'You may indeed, Adam,' Em said, turning her cheek for his kiss. 'You even precede my husband who hasn't yet felt obliged to do so.'

'Oh, Em, do not say that. I intended to, first thing but...'

'But you didn't. Here, Adam, would you like to hold the babe?'

I watched Adam lift the babe as though he had done it a hundred times, so confident, it was galling.

'Hey, little man,' he crooned. 'Welcome to the world. See here, my finger to hold. I'll say, Seb, he has the grip of a miser on his money. A fine strong lad, I think.'

Perversely, I was glad when the babe began to wail, proving Adam was not so skilled with infants as he pretended. But he made shushing noises and rocked it in the crook of one arm and it quieted. I would not have known what to do.

'Perhaps, you should go to your Mam for an early dinnertime, eh?' Adam suggested, as if he expected the babe to say aye or nay. Such foolishness. 'Come, there's a fine little fellow.' He handed the babe back to Em who, without the least concern for propriety, bared her breast and held the babe close.

I turned away from such intimacy but saw Adam did not, so I took his arm and pulled him outside.

'There be no need to stare at my wife.'

'Stare? Oh, I understand. You think only you may see her tits. Not so in this village, Seb, however 'tis done in the city. Here, all the mothers feed their babes whenever 'tis needful. You've seen Luke's wife do it often enough. Why should they hide away? When a babe howls because it's hungry, 'tis a relief to us all to see it fed.'

That was the truth but whenever I saw a woman half unclothed, whatever the reason, I had manners enough to look elsewhere. But then I realised, when a family lived in a single room, a woman had no choice, so everyone was used to seeing the intimacy of suckling a babe. In London, it was the custom for women to withdraw, but here, that was impossible.

'Forgive me, Adam. I did not intend to be sharp with you. I realise such a scene be commonplace to you.'

'Aye, but you were right. I was staring. Your Emily is beautiful. You best guard her well, else your cousin will be after eating forbidden fruit.'

'Cousin Luke? Surely not?'

'He has the morals of a goat and the strength of a stallion. You can't have failed to hear the rumours.'

'Well, no. I heard them but...'

'They're not just rumours, Seb.'

Cousin Joan served our dinner – the rabbit stew we should have enjoyed yesterday – and then left to go home, taking young Mary and promising to return later. Thinking on it, I realised Joan had most likely been up all night long, aiding Em. She must be tired.

Em settled the babe in its borrowed crib and joined Adam and me at the board. I discovered I was famished and we all ate heartily. I fear Gawain's share was less than usual, we were all so hungry and the stew was excellent. I wiped my bowl spotlessly clean with a corner of bread. Adam did the same, then retrieved a last crumb from his beard.

'That was a fine dinner,' he said. 'Now I must be away to the manor – a whole morning's worth of lists to catch up on. Shall I see you at the tavern after work, Seb, as usual?'

'No, I think not. I'm drinking only water for now.'

'Wise, indeed,' he chuckled. 'You should have seen your man last eve, Emily...'

'Better that she did not,' I said quickly.

'Why? What did he do?' Em gave me such a look.

'Besides,' I said, 'My goodwife and I must deliberate upon a name for our child. That be of greater importance. And then I must arrange godparents and the baptism for the morrow.'

'You may tell me later,' Em told Adam, which boded ill for me.

We were finally alone: our little family. It felt strange to realise it was no longer just us two. We had a child to consider every day, every hour for the rest of our lives. Such a change was alarming to me.

'I've already asked your Cousin Joan to stand as his godmother,' Em said. 'It's up to you to ask the godfathers.'

'Adam has offered.'

'I suppose he's as good as anyone. What about Cousin Luke? He's always so generous in bringing us game for the pot and wood for the fire.'

'No. Not him,' I said hastily.

'Why not? You haven't quarrelled with him, have you, Seb?'

'Of course not. 'Tis just I thought someone else would be more suitable. Luke has enough of his own children to raise.' I remembered what Adam said about those rumours being true. It also made me wonder about the reason for Luke's generosity. Did he have an eye for my Em, too? But I was being uncharitable.

'Who did you have in mind?'

'Er, Cousin Bayard has standing in the village, being the steward of the manor.'

'We don't know him very well though, do we? What of your brother, Thomas, or Cousin John?'

'Aye, maybe. 'Tis a pity we cannot defer the appointment of a second godfather until we return to London. I would so wish it could be Jude.' To console myself, missing Jude deeply of a sudden, I bent and ruffled Gawain's soft coat, stroking his ears.

'Well, you can't. Our son needs to be baptised now, not next year sometime. But what of a name? Have you thought much on this?' Em paused and looked at me straightly. 'You haven't given it a moment's consideration, have you?'

'I have.'

'Sebastian Foxley, you never can tell me a lie that I don't recognise at once for what it is. You turn red as a rosehip the instant the words leave your mouth.'

'I have been trying to think on it, Em, but I've had the mural to work on and...' My excuse was lamer than a three-legged donkey. 'I'm sorry. Let us think on it now. You once suggested Stephen, after your father. And I recall you mentioning Edward for the king.'

'Stephen is a fine name, but with two in the family, we may confuse which one we mean in conversation.'

'I doubt it. Your father will never be needing his tail-clout changing, nor the babe to take an order for new fence palings. Other families manage. Think of my grandsire, Bayard Armitage and Uncle Bayard and Cousin Bayard: they do well enough. We'll call him Stephen.'

'No. I like the name, but he doesn't look like a Stephen.' Em was thoughtful and sipped her dinnertime ale.

'Edward, then. Little Ned. Ned Foxley.'

'No. I used to like the name, but I've changed my mind.'

'Nicholas. Thomas, after the apostle in the church here. Or John, after Father Haughton. I don't know, Em. What about Richard, after the duke as my patron?'

'Aye, that's a good name. But what about Lord Richard's brother?'

'You just said you changed your mind about Edward.'

'Not the king; the other one.'

'Oh, no, Em, not George. That name brings back too many dark memories of the Tower for me.'

'Of course, not George. The other brother. The one Lord Richard had you paint his image for the triptych. You remember? His likeness looked very handsome. What was his name?'

'The Earl of Rutland. Aye, Edmund, it was. You like that name?'

'Edmund Foxley. I think that sounds very well indeed. What do you think, Seb?'

'Well, it rolls pleasantly off my tongue: Edmund Foxley. He might get called 'Mundy'. Would you mind that?'

'No, I quite like that too. So, 'tis settled then. We'll call him Edmund.' I saw her hesitating, fingering her chin. 'Unless you prefer Richard?'

'Lord save us, woman! Are you changing your mind yet again? I never thought choosing a name could be so arduous.'

'Richard Foxley. I like that better maybe.'

I put my head in my hands and sighed.

'Richard it shall be, then,' I said.

'No, no. This decision can't be rushed, Seb. Edmund? Richard? Richard? Edmund? Or Edward? Maybe that is better yet?'

'Spare me, Em!' I threw up my hands in despair. 'I'm going to the church to ask Father John about arranging the baptism.'

'Aye, John is a good name...'

'You have until then to decide, else we'll call him Aristotle and be done with it.'

'Aristotle? Aye, he'd never be confused with anyone else then. Aristotle Foxley...'

Some hours later, with the baptismal ceremony arranged for the vespers office on the morrow, and suppertime proving a tortuous ordeal with Em suckling the babe at table and all the while arguing with herself over the poor mite's name, I changed my mind about meeting Adam at the Nether End Tavern.

'How are you enjoying fatherhood then?' he asked, gesturing at Uncle Harry Oakenshaw to bring me ale.

28

''Tis fraught, indeed. I left Em debating a name.'

'With herself?'

'Aye. She has arguments enough for an entire guild meeting. She doesn't need my contribution. At present, the last I heard, it was going to require the toss of a coin to choose betwixt Humphrey and Lancelot.' I slumped upon the bench beside Adam and Gawain flopped down upon my feet as usual. He used to sleep betwixt them when he was small but now made use of them as a pillow.

'Wetting the babe's head, are we, Seb?' Cousin Luke pulled up a stool and John did likewise – ever his elder brother's silent shadow.

'Only with water, in my case,' I told him, waving away the ale jug.

'Oh, come now. We have to drink to little whatshisname,' Luke insisted. 'And what is his name?'

I said naught.

'Lancelot,' Adam announced in a loud voice that carried across the room and out through the open door, into the warm evening airs.

'What!' Luke sprayed his mouthful of ale, spluttering with laughter. 'Is that the sort of name Londoners give their babes? No wonder England is going to the dogs. Begging Gawain's pardon.' He patted my dog who thumped his tail in approval.

The tavern customers were rolling about, snorting with merriment.

'Always knew them Londoners was mad as March hares,' someone called out. A Rudd, I believe it was, one of Aunt Marjorie's other relations, or maybe a Parfitt.

'For nigh unto an hour this afternoon, it was going to be Aristotle,' I admitted. 'I think Lancelot be an improvement on that at least.'

Adam climbed up onto the bench, holding his cup high.

'Everybody!' he shouted. 'Raise your cups to our newest soul in the village: Aristotle Armit...'

I pulled him off his perch, spilling his ale.

'Be quiet Adam, for pity's sake. I told you it isn't determined yet.'

'But we haven't had such a fine jest since Uncle Bayard fell in the mud and lost his feathered cap to a passing nanny goat a month since. We be in need of a hearty laugh, Seb, and you must agree that Aristotle Armitage is as fine a one as could be.'

'That is not my son's name,' I exclaimed, leaping to my feet. 'Don't make a laughing matter of it, any of you. Not you, Adam, nor Cousin Luke, nor any of you Rudds and Parfitts. You hear me! We are calling him Richard, after His Grace, the Duke of Gloucester, King Edward's brother and *my* patron. And don't you dare mock him!'

There was a long silence. What had I done, making known a name without Em's approval? She would never forgive me, but the die was cast now. Then the whole company was on its feet – including Uncle Oakenshaw – raising their cups and shouting my son's name, drinking his health. 'Wassail, Little Dickon, son of Seb Armitage of Foxley!' they cried as one. Of a sudden, the babe had its parentage and origin proclaimed. There was no undoing it: he was accepted as a villager by birthright, just as I must once have been. And I was glad of it too, that he was no more London born than I was, ordained by Fate, as it must have been, for we never intended it so.

Gradually, the company settled once more, like a henhouse after the fox has passed by, though my back was slapped in congratulation so many times, I was certain I must have bruises to show for it. Many would buy me ale, but I steadfastly refused anything but stream water. Not so Adam, who happily drained any ale cup set before me, saying I might thus avoid giving offence to well-meaning friends and neighbours. He was welcome to it after my sufferings last eve and this morn.

Cousin Luke left us to pursue his favoured quarry of the moment: young Meg Rudd, the pretty tavern wench in Uncle Oakenshaw's employ. Luke had been regaling us for some days, weeks, concerning Meg's undoubted well-rounded 'assets'. I could not say how far the chase had gone, but this eve, Luke appeared intent upon bringing down his prey at last. The lass did not seem unwilling either, brushing him close as she squeezed by him, though there was room enough and to spare. I noticed that at some point, the lacings at the top of her gown had come loose and not by mischance, I was sure.

'His Cecily used to be just as buxom, poor lass,' Adam said, watching the tavern wench enticing Luke, 'Until he wore her out with so many babes in so few years.'

'Five? With the eldest, what, ten summers old? Is that too many?' I asked.

'Oh, probably not, if that were all. But she lost babes in between, miscarrying them or else they were born too soon. Another died at a few months of age. 'Tis not a merry tale, Seb.'

'Little wonder then that she looks so thin and wan, poor Cis. I did not know.'

At that moment, Luke took Meg in his bear-like embrace, over in the corner, and kissed her hard. She made little attempt to fight him off but whether because she welcomed him or because his strength made any such effort futile, was hard to tell. If she would cry out, his kisses smothered any sounds.

But one of the Parfitts – Nicholas – had no doubts. He had a cudgel in hand, the one Uncle Oakenshaw kept by for restoring order among drunkards of a Saturday eve if need arose. Nicholas flew across the room and brought it down with a mighty thwack across Luke's shoulders. We all winced under that blow. It would have been a cracked skull for my cousin, had he not been so tall that Nicholas could not reach.

'I'll not have you deflower my Meg, Luke Forester, as you deflower other wenches, you filthy animal. We're to be wed and I won't stand for it.' The blows rained down, but Luke seemed little inconvenienced by them. He released Meg and turned slowly to face Nicholas, a fellow half his size who still had the cudgel raised, threateningly.

'Put that down afore you hurt yourself,' Luke said, grinning. He prised the weapon out of the younger man's grasp with ease and threw it aside to crash upon the floor. 'You be a foolish fellow, Nick, if you think you may preserve the honour of every wench in the parish. Besides, they enjoy it, see?' He crushed Meg close against him. She smiled. Or it may have been a grimace – it was hard to tell. 'Go back to tending your bean-patch and stop trying to play the knight, riding to rescue every maiden, even when they're not in distress.'

That seemed to be the end of it and everyone returned to their cups and conversation yet what I saw then was quite shocking. I nudged Adam to look at Nicholas Parfitt as he retrieved the club and went for Luke again. Was he quite mad? He caught Luke across the small of his back where even such a giant had a vulnerable spot.

Luke cursed in pain and turned, spitting anger. He seized the cudgel and brought it down with all his strength, demolishing a table board and a bench. The weapon also broke, stout as it was and impossible as it seemed. It could so easily have been Nicholas's brains scattered among the rushes, instead of splinters of wood. But Luke wasn't done yet. He roared like a bull and charged, even as his would-be attacker tried to flee. Uncle Oakenshaw's yells to desist went unheard.

Determined to even the odds and prevent bloodshed, if I could, I hastily put a stool in his path and Luke went sprawling. Adam and I and a half dozen other fellows piled on top of him, yet he still tried to fight us all off, fists and feet flailing. Bennett Rudd, Nicholas's second or step-cousin, I was unsure which, was knocked senseless; another of the Parfitts was bleeding from a broken nose and Adam's lip was split. I was kicked on the knee and thumped in the ribs, but as to who did the damage, I had no idea in the melée.

We were still lying in a heap with Luke writhing beneath, attempting to heave us off, when Steward Bayard made his entrance, proud and haughty as any lord. No doubt, we made a fine sight, all of us bloodied, bruised and groaning in a squirming mass. Steward Bayard glanced down, bestowing a look of glaring contempt upon us, afore stepping around us as some unsavoury nastiness to be avoided at all cost. He surely knew how to make a man feel of less importance than a worm.

'Cease!' the steward roared. Gradually, the noise died away and we began to disentangle ourselves, inspecting the damage inflicted upon both our bodies and clothing. We were none of us an edifying sight. 'Hear me, all you malefactors,' Steward Bayard announced with a sneer, thumping the floor with his staff of office, 'Upon the morrow, you men will bring your scythes to the hayfield. Haymaking time is at hand. Latecomers will be fined. And next week, you'll come up to the manor. There is work to be done to prepare for a bridal party. Women to weed the courtyard; men to limewash the walls.'

'You can't make us do that: 'tis not boon work according to our tenancy holding. Haymaking be one thing, but we're not fancying up the manor house, wedding or no wedding.' The speaker was Adam, bold as ever.

Steward Bayard's face was terrible as he confronted Adam. They were nigh nose to nose, but Adam did not back down.

'Ever the troublemaker, Armitage? You best watch your step.'

'Adam be right, though,' Cousin Luke said, standing at Adam's shoulder. He had finally managed to free himself from the pile of would-be peacekeepers but now sported a monstrous black eye and a gash across his cheek which bled still. 'You watch your step, steward. We don't take kindly to those who overstep their office.'

'Be off,' Uncle Oakenshaw cried. 'Get to your homes. There's been trouble enough here this eve. Upon the morrow, I shall be demanding recompense for the damage done. Now, go. Tavern's closed.'

Steward Bayard was the first out the door, not that he hastened for that was beneath his dignity and might even give the false impression that he was obeying Uncle Oakenshaw's order. That would never do. The rest of us collected our wits along with our scattered caps and discarded jerkins. In some cases, we made our apologies, as I did to both Uncle Oakenshaw and Cousin Luke. Others did not: most notably, Nicholas Parfitt said naught to Luke but scowled at him ferociously as he led Meg Rudd away. No liking there, for certain. Neither did Luke apologise to anyone for wrecking the tavern, nor to Meg for mishandling her, if indeed he saw it that way.

It was fortunate that I had survived the brawl intact but for a few bruises which did not show. Otherwise, I would have had to explain to Em what came to pass at the tavern and that was not advisable. Bad enough that I must tell her I had named our son without her consent. I hoped the rent seam in my shirt might go unnoticed for this night at least. I bade Adam 'good night', though the sun was not yet set this close to midsummer, and advised him to put a cold compress upon his split and swollen lip. He laughed and said he'd had far worse hurts than that. We parted company at my door and I paused to brace myself afore entering and pushed the door open.

Em sprung towards me.

'I've decided upon his name, Seb,' she declared, seizing my arm and dragging me to the crib. 'Look at him sleeping. I have chosen the perfect name for the perfect child.'

My heart sank at her excitement, aware the babe was already irrevocably named.

'We shall call him Richard: a princely name indeed. Don't you agree, husband?'

'Richard? You be certain?' Relief flowed through me such that I had to sit, my knees gone weak.

'You don't like my choice?' she asked, a prickly tone creeping into her voice.

'I heartily approve, Em. 'Tis a fine and most suitable name. I love it.' I pulled her onto my lap and held her close against my heart. 'And I love the lass who gave me such son. Thank you, Em, for everything.' I kissed her tenderly, her lips sweet against mine, noticing over her shoulder the bunch of roses and wildflowers I had picked for her yesterday in a pot beside the bed.

Chapter 3

Wednesday, the seventeenth day of June

I WAS AT St Thomas's Church right early, eager to make up for time lost yesterday. I was behind in my work. This morn, I had prepared more yellow ochre, binding it with the yolk of a hen's egg, needing just a little to complete the fires of Hell, low down upon the figure of Christ's left hand. I was pleased with the redone image of Christ in Majesty: none need know how close was the new likeness to the portrait I had done of the Duke of Gloucester, that expression of authority tinged with compassion that was so familiar to me from intimate study of my subject – a liberty only permitted to an artist and, mayhap, a physician.

I moved away, as far as the scaffold boards allowed, to view the overall effect. Did Hell appear sufficiently hellish to deter sinners? I thought it did. Two final brushstrokes and I stopped, rinsed out my brushes and set them to dry. Next, I took the white of the egg, leftover from preparing the ochre, and mixed it with the azurite I had ground ready last eve, after we were told to leave the tavern. Egg white was better for mixing blues, avoiding the yellowness imparted by the yolk that would turn the blue to green. The previous unknown limner, who had painted this wonderful mural more than a hundred years ago, depicted the blessed souls climbing a golden ladder towards Heaven, escorted by angels clad in blue robes. He may have used lapis lazuli since the colour of the robes had lasted well, except for an area where the damp had crept in. This, I intended to retouch with the azurite for I had used up the last of my precious lapis in repainting Christ's royal gown, adding crimson lake to the shadows in the folds of drapery to give a purple hue, fit for the King of Heaven.

Uncle Oakenshaw came into the church as usual at this time. I greeted him and Gawain gave him a friendly woof of welcome but, as ever, Harry Oakenshaw was a man of few words. He stood watching me for a few minutes, shaking his head and sniffing his disapproval, though of what he disapproved – me or my work or some other thing – I could not tell. He went to his private prayers and departed soon after. But he was not our only visitor.

I had just completed the thorough mixing of the azurite, achieving the required consistency, and was choosing my brush when the latch on the great oaken door rattled in its hasp a second time. Gawain gave no welcome to the newcomer but rather a low growl.

'Quiet, Gawain,' I told him, turning to see who it was that my dog had so little liking for. It was Steward Bayard, no less. 'God give you good day, sir,' I called down to him, hoping my courtesy would serve to placate any ill-humour of his. I know not why my uncles and cousins on my father's side of the family appeared to suffer so from discontentment when my mother's relatives were a merry crowd for the most part.

'Get down from there now,' he barked, not wasting words on a greeting.

'Forgive me, but my work be at a critical point, sir. I cannot leave this fresh mixed pigment, else it will be wasted.'

'I said "now!", you insolent pup and don't dare defy me.'

'Very well but I must cover the pot with a wet cloth first, then it will keep a while at least.' Then, with my customary caution, I descended the ladder from my high perch. 'How may I serve you, sir?' I asked when I reached the nave floor and stood facing him, hoping my irritation at being dragged from my work was not so obvious to him. I noted that he looked flushed indeed, though whether from wearing a furred robe on such a warm day or because he was angered, I was uncertain.

'You can serve your lord by getting out to the hayfield and doing the work you owe according to your terms of tenancy. You were in the tavern last eve; you heard what I told all the rest, so how come you think to disobey me, eh?' Steward Bayard pushed his face so close to mine that I could feel the heat from his skin and smell his unsavoury breath.

'I am not disobeying you, sir,' I said, taking a step back. 'When I first came here and we discussed my tenancy of the cottage, it was agreed that, since I have never worked the land in my life and being somewhat afflicted in my hip, my Forester cousins would do my share of labouring and, in exchange, I would make good this mural at my own expense. That was what we determined, sir.'

'That was then; this is now. We be short-handed, what with one of the Parfitts run off, a Persloe with a broken arm and Old Man Rudd being likely upon his deathbed. You will do your share, same as everyone else. Come. I have a scythe to spare.' He grabbed my arm and Gawain growled threateningly. 'Call off your damned dog, or I'll have it destroyed.'

'Hush, Gawain, lad. All is well,' I said, patting his silky head. But all was not well. The steward dragged me from my work and would not leave hold of me, forcing me across the way like a recalcitrant schoolboy and down betwixt two cottages, into the hayfield beyond. At the field's edge, he shoved a scythe into my pigment-stained hands and bade me get to my labours. I looked at him and then at the heavy implement I held. I had not the least idea how to use it.

The line of labourers had already worked its way down the field somewhat. All wore their sleeves rolled up and hats of woven straw to keep off the sun. Above us, in the azure vault of the sky, a lark sang his little heart out in a hymn of praise. And here was I, staring dumbfounded at the unwieldy blade I was supposed to employ.

'Get on with it, you useless fool, else your cottage will be repossessed at sunset. See how they do it? Swing from the hips, not the shoulders.'

I hefted the scythe – heavy indeed – and did a first tentative swing of the blade. A line of fine grass and a moon daisy fell before me.

'Wider sweeps than that, else there'll be stuff left uncut betwixt you and the reapers either side. Now get moving. You be far behind as it is.'

I tried again, sweeping a broader arc.

'Wider!' he roared.

This time, I almost overbalanced.

'Feet well apart, you useless toad.'

I did as he said and felt the bones and sinews of my left hip protesting at the unaccustomed movement.

'Now put your back into it. Get a rhythm going: sweep, step, return, sweep, step, return. That's it.'

I managed a couple of sweeps, missing a tuft of ryegrass and having to go back. Then I caught my foot in a depression – a half-dug rabbit hole – and ended up on my backside, the scythe blade wavering dangerously close by my shin.

'Get up! You damned fool. Wider sweeps, a smooth swing.'

I clambered awkwardly to my feet, sweating like a pig on a spit, my hair clinging to my face and getting in my eyes. Now I knew why country folk wore their hair short. I calmed myself by breathing deep and taking a moment to listen to the skylark's song. At least he was happy. A sudden cuff about my ear reminded me what I was supposed to be about. Gawain snarled and I bade him be quiet for I feared losing him as well as the cottage.

I began again, sensing the steward there behind me, out of harm's way but close enough to clout me if he thought I was slacking. My progress was an agony: not only did it proceed more slowly than a snail's pace but my hip screeched for mercy at every swing of the scythe. My face was not only awash with perspiration, but there were tears also. My hands were likewise slippery with sweat, such that it made my grip uncertain and I frequently paused to wipe them on my breeches for fear of an accident. One time, as I did this, I realised it left a red smear. My palms were blistered and bleeding already and it was not yet dinnertime. My tongue stuck to my palate and my lips were baked and cracking, stinging from my salt sweat. How was I to live 'til dinner? My attention was wandering and I mistimed a sweep and fell, narrowly avoiding the blade again, though the tip caught my calf, slit my breeches and drew a little blood.

The steward made no comment, but I expected another blow. When none was forthcoming, I looked back. I had achieved about ten, maybe fifteen yards or so of unevenly cut hay that was barely worth the pain and effort but what angered me most was the sight of Steward Bayard propped against the hedge, his hat pulled down over his eyes, sleeping like the blessed.

Cursing him, I resumed my work, of whatever poor quality, until black spots began to appear at the edge of my vision. Stopping for a moment, I looked up and suddenly saw, nay felt, the world tipping sideways. Dizzy, I laid aside the scythe and sat down amid the stubble to wait for the world to steady itself.

'Seb. What in St Thomas's holy name are you doing here? Look at the state of you. Come, sit in the shade. You didn't ought to be out with no hat to keep the sun off. And where be your water flask? Have you drunk anything since you've been here?' Adam hauled me to my feet and guided me as I staggered towards the shade of the hedge. 'What were you thinking of, eh? Was it not decided that labouring wasn't for you? That was agreed, was it not? Why did you come, all unprepared like this? Here, have my water. Drink it slow now.'

My saviour handed me his water bottle. Sun-warmed water had never tasted so marvellous. A few more mouthfuls and I began to revive.

'I had no choice. Steward Bayard threatened to take the roof from over our heads if I did not. Oh, Adam, I've never worked so hard in my life. A whole day of this will slay me. Look at my hands. Heaven knows how long they will take to heal.'

'That man be the Devil's own taskmaster, but we'll remind him, Luke, John and I, that we said we would do your share in the fields. No more labouring for you, Seb, if indeed you can yet stand on your own two feet. The matter seems in question, looking at you just now.'

'I feel much improved and I thank you for it.'

'Aye. Well, the women will be out with our bread and ale soon,' Adam said, squinting up at the sky, now brassy with heat as the sun climbed to its zenith. Even the lark had abandoned his singing to seek some cool bower. 'We all get to rest for an hour then.' He glanced at the steward, still dozing, and scowled. 'Wore himself out, watching others work, no doubt. Luke will have something to say on that score.'

We were the first to notice two groups of women and children approaching, one coming from the Upper End of The Street, the other from the Nether End – our end. They were chattering and laughing together. I caught a snatch of song from our women. The men ceased their work and all came to join the women and youngsters in the shade of the hedge and the shadow of a small copse, edged by three large oaks. The women handed out wedges of bread and hard cheese, then went about with ale flagons and water buckets. Em was not with them and I realised she would be at home, expecting my return for dinner. I would have to send a message with one of the children or suffer the consequences of upsetting her. It was the case that, having laboured together in the lord's field all morn, the folk from The Street beyond the church kept to themselves and we did the same. I knew very few Upper Enders by their Christian names, even after three months.

Cousin Luke came over to where Adam and I lay at our ease among moon daisies and buttercups at the field margin, laughing at Gawain's attempts to herd the brown speckled butterflies dancing in the sun. Eventually, the dog gave up, snapped at a few flies instead and flopped down panting, his tongue lolling and dripping. When Luke's wife, Cecily, brought us the water bucket, I took the chance to splash my face as well as drink before making certain Gawain had water also.

'Never thought to see you here, cousin,' she said. 'Your Emily was preparing pease pottage for you when I saw her earlier.'

'I never thought to be here either, Cecily. Would one of your youngsters go tell her I shall not be home quite yet, please?'

I noticed Nicholas Parfitt and Meg Rudd sitting just a little apart from the rest of us, kissing and smiling. It seemed Cousin Luke's actions last eve, having forced Nick to reveal his attachment to the lass, had now granted them licence to be together openly. They made a good couple by the look of it.

As the women collected up the empty cups and bread baskets, the men took their ease, some talking and jesting, others dozing or taking a whetstone to resharpen their scythe blades, as Adam did. A few went off into the copse to answer nature's call or to seek deeper shade. Uncle Harry Oakenshaw sat inspecting the handle of his scythe, as if it might have developed a splinter. Every man had his own implement adapted to his liking and suited to his height and build, each marked for ownership. The one I had been using had a double cross carved into the handle.

'Damned fool,' Adam said when he noticed the mark. 'Did Steward Bayard give you this?'

I nodded.

'Aye. He said it was spare.'

'This be Old Man Rudd's and he but half your height and twice as broad. No wonder you were having trouble with it. The handle be far too short for you and weighted all wrong.' He showed me his own, marked with three roughly overlapping circles. 'See the strips of lead around the handle? They're to balance it just how I find most comfortable to use. Surely

Bayard couldn't have thought that one was right for you? He's an imbecile if he did.'

'On your feet, you idle dogs,' Steward Bayard shouted. 'Back to work, all of you.'

I was unsurprised when he came striding toward Adam and me. I could well suppose what he was about to say.

'You too, you London lick-spittle. Pick up the scythe.'

'No,' I said. 'My hands be so blistered, I can do no more.'

'Then you know the consequences, as I warned you earlier.'

'There will be no consequences,' Adam told him, getting to his feet in a single fluid movement I could never match. 'We witnessed the agreement betwixt you, Luke Forester and me when Seb first came here. You agreed that for a purse full of coin – which you were all too eager to accept – and Luke, his brother and I promising to do his share, Seb would be spared the labour dues that he cannot perform. You agreed to that, knowing his work is penmanship and artistry, not pruning and reaping. 'Tis a miracle he hasn't hacked off a limb, either his own or someone else's.'

'I made no such agreement,' the steward began, but Adam grabbed a handful of his furred robe.'

'Indeed you did, you worm. Where's Luke? He was there to witness it. Luke! Answer me, you deaf dolt!'

We looked around at the men retrieving their scythes and getting ready to begin work once more. I could not see Luke among them and one his size would be hard to miss.

'Cousin Cecily!' I called. 'Where be your goodman?'

'I'm not sure. Last I saw of him, he went into the copse to piss. Mayhap, he be down the field already. I be off home. I'll give Emily your message as I pass by.'

'My thanks for that, cousin.' Just because I was no longer going to cut hay did not mean my work was done for the day. I would return to the church and do my best to rescue the azurite pigment I had prepared earlier, but Steward Bayard had other ideas and would make an argument of it.

'You will take a sickle then,' he told me, holding out a far smaller implement – one I did know how to use for even in London clumps of nettles needed cutting back and bindweed had to be removed occasionally. 'Cut at the field margin what the reapers have to leave with the large blades for fear of damaging the hedges.' His face was implacable. 'Do it.'

With reluctance, I was about to accept the sickle, but Adam snatched it away.

'How many times does it need be said?' he yelled at the steward. 'Seb has paid you *in lieu* of work. I'll find Luke and he'll put you straight on this matter, you devil, with his fists, if necessary, and as the lord's forester, you'll have no right to threaten his house. Come, Seb, let's find him. I cannot see him in the field and Cecily said he went into the copse. Mayhap the rogue found a wandering wench there to delay his return.'

'To work, the pair of you, or else...' the steward screeched, grabbing my shirt but Gawain growled and sprung at him and I pulled free. The thought of having Gawain and both Adam and Luke to champion my cause gave me heart indeed. I shielded my eyes from the sun's glare and surveyed the field: men from up The Street were working over the far side. Luke would not be there among the Persloes, Meades and Butts but neither could I make out his great form amidst our own. Adam's father, Uncle Thomas Armitage; Uncle Oakenshaw; Cousin John; Bennett Rudd; his brothers and Nicholas Parfitt were all there in the line of reapers, rhythmically swinging their blades, but not Cousin Luke.

'You be right, Adam. I see no sign of Luke either and it be unlike him to shirk his labours.'

'Unlike you idle curs,' the steward snarled, but Gawain's snarl was the more threatening. 'I'll string up that accursed animal of yours, too.' Despite his words, the man backed away.

Ignoring the steward, Adam and I, with Gawain at my side, went into the copse, calling Luke's name to warn him, if he was with a wench. The trees enclosed us in their verdant shade. It was cool here and quiet but for the buzz of flies and the softest rustle of a breeze, stirring the leaves in the canopy high above. We trod softly on the moss and damp leaf mould of the woodland floor, like stepping on velvet.

Further in, even the flies and wind fell silent. Too silent. I felt the hairs on the back of my neck tingling. Gawain stopped, ears pricked forward. Adam looked at me and I could see he sensed it also. I bent down and whispered to my dog:

'Gawain. Go find Cousin Luke.' I did not know whether Gawain understood, being still but a pup if a well-grown one, but if neither sight nor sound of Luke were apparent to us, mayhap his scent would be to a more sensitive nose. After a few moments of looking at me with his lustrous brown eyes, head on one side, as if attempting to understand some foreign tongue, Gawain put his wet snout to the earth and began questing around for some familiar scent.

'Is he good at following a trail?' Adam asked, sounding doubtful.

'I've never tried him 'til now. Who can say what a dog makes of the world, but he be as likely as we to find Luke, even by chance.'

'You think something bad has happened.'

I was unsure if Adam was asking me or stating a fact but I shrugged rather than make answer. Gawain seemed to have found a scent and moved on. Mayhap, he was following the trail of a fox or badger or some other woodland creature, but we followed all the same. He trotted off betwixt the trees, circled a large oak and then, of a sudden, stopped and came back to us, giving an uncertain little yip, as if asking me what he should do next. A cold finger of sweat trickled down my spine. I swallowed hard.

'What have you found, lad?' I said, fearing that I knew. There was a strange sound here, an insistent low hum and a faint smell that did not belong to the green wood. Slowly, I approached the broad trunk of a mighty oak. The hum grew louder; the odour stronger. I closed my eyes in a brief moment of prayer afore walking around the tree. The hum of swarming flies and the stink of blood was a reminder of the butchers' Shambles back in London.

'Dear Christ!' Adam groaned and turned away to vomit, steadying himself against a neighbouring tree.

We had found Cousin Luke.

I knelt beside him, shocked to discover that he breathed still, if barely. I took his hand in mine and spoke his name.

'Cousin Luke, 'tis me, Seb. Who did this to you, Luke? Tell me.'

His eyes flickered open. I waved away the flies that tormented him, attracted already to his grievous wounds. Luke could not speak, but he put out his other hand, clawing at the leaves that lay upon the woodland floor. I thought it was a spasm of pain that caused this yet he chose a single leaf from those he clutched and gave it to me. A parting gift, so it seemed, for blood trickled from his mouth, bubbling with one last breath. Then Luke was gone. No prayers. No confession. No absolution. No comfort. Just gone.

'By God's life. How do we tell his poor wife?' Adam said, coming to stand beside me, his gaze averted still.

'We must fetch the priest,' I told him, for a moment unable to recall the cleric's name, so benumbed were my thought processes. 'Gawain. Come away now!' I would not have my dog sniffing at my cousin.

'I'll go. And I'll inform Steward Bayard on the way.' Adam ran back towards the field, eager to be elsewhere. I could not blame him. I, too, wished myself anywhere but here yet Luke must not be left for fear foxes or stray curs might do him further insult. I closed his eyes and wiped away the blood from his lips where flies clustered dark against his skin. I murmured the prayer for the dead, learned by rote through years of copying out service books and attending funerals. They were empty words now. There could be no consolation for this.

I know not how long it took – time meant little. It could have been moments or hours but the sun, blinking through the trees above, was still high when they came: Adam, Father John Haughton and Steward Bayard with a crowd at their backs, following on. The priest was plainly shocked, but it was the steward who reeled, upon the verge of swooning. I continued my kneeling vigil, waving away the flies as they tried to settle.

'This be bloody murder.' Having composed himself, the steward stated the obvious in a quivering monotone. 'Who did this?' Did he expect someone to step forward and confess? No one spoke. The gathering was stunned into silence. Then Cousin John came and knelt beside me. Though tears coursed down his sun-browned cheeks, he remained silent in sorrow as the priest began the solemn rites. Behind me now, I heard voices raised, but I gave them no mind. My thoughts were all for the cousin I had come to love.

When the rites were ended, the priest stepped aside and two fellows came with a woven withy hurdle and a folded blanket. They set the hurdle down and spread the blanket upon it.

I held out my hand to Adam to help me rise for my hip refused to oblige at first. It took four of us to lift Luke – myself and Adam, Cousin John and the priest – a final service for my cousin. We lowered him onto the hurdle with the utmost care and then I covered him, tucking in the blanket as if securing a child in bed. I realised then that others would have to carry the dear burden to St Thomas's for my strength was spent. I sat beneath a tree and stared at naught.

It was my faithful Gawain who restored my wits, nudging me and licking at my hand. The sun was lower in the sky now and a chill breeze had picked up, rustling the leafy canopy above. I realised I felt cold as I clambered to my feet with much difficulty, stiff from sitting so long. In truth, I didn't want to move, to rejoin the world where I would be required to act, to speak, to answer questions. Where should I go? To the church, maybe? Or to Aunt Marjorie, to break the fearful tidings to her and poor Cecily? No. That was Cousin John's task. Or the priest's. Home, then. Aye. But should I tell Em of the dreadful happenings? Had I not read or heard somewhere that the shock of ill news could curdle a woman's breast milk? How could I speak gently of such matters so as not to affright her? That I should have to tell her was not in doubt, for she would hear of it else wise, from some other, if I did not.

I might have spared myself the anxiety on the walk home, rehearsing the words to myself in an attempt to lessen the horrors, for Adam was seated at the board with my wife, sharing ale, when I walked through the open door. Their sombre looks were sufficient: Adam had told her already. I patted his shoulder in silent gratitude, certain he had made a better job of it than I could have done.

Emily poured me some ale, saying naught. Then she fetched a ladle of hot water from a pot on the fire and put it in the laver bowl, adding cold water from the bucket by the door. The message was clear: I needed to wash. Only as the water discoloured did I notice my hands were stained with blood. My jerkin and shirt also. My cousin's blood. It was then that the tears began. I could not hold them back but wept like a little maid. If I longed for comfort, it came in a strange way. I dried both my tears and my hands on a cloth and removed my soiled clothing, as Em told me. I half expected a scolding for the state of my attire and the work that would ensue in getting it clean. Instead, Emily handed me the swaddled bundle that was my little son.

'One comes into this world and one goes out – how often is that the way of it?' Em said. 'This little one is your consolation, Seb. Don't weep now. He is to be christened at vespers, remember? You need to prepare.' Ever practical, she would not waste time on grief when there were things to be done.

As was ever the way, the babe's mother would not attend the ceremony, she being banned from social gatherings until she was churched. Thus, it was my responsibility to gather the godparents and take my son to the font. Though I was hardly of a humour for such a joyous event, I needs must put on a merry countenance for his sake. I wondered whether Cousin Joan would feel up to performing the office of godmother, but I soon learned that these Norfolk relatives of mine were cut from stout cloth indeed. I was about to walk over to Aunt Marjorie's cottage, reluctant to intrude so soon after they had learned of Luke's death, when the Forester women arrived at our door, all but Mistress Cecily at least. Understandably, being newly widowed, she would want to be with her children, sitting quietly. They were somewhat red-eyed but cleanly and neatly clad in their Sunday best – a credit to their inner strength and resolve. I too must make an effort then.

'Cecily and the children will be along shortly, to give your Emily company,' Aunt Marjorie said. 'Better that she not be alone just now,' she added in a whisper for my ears only, and I knew not whether she meant my Emily or poor Cecily, or both, mayhap.

I nodded, feeling ashamed of my earlier weakness when compared to the fortitude of those to whom Luke's passing meant so much more as a son, a brother, a husband and a father and, not least, a loss of livelihood also. Who was I to bow my head and shed useless tears when they held their heads high and wore their shock and grief as bravely as a knight wears his armour?

I could not fault the women's conduct throughout the office of vespers, nor my son's christening that followed. If a tear escaped an eye, which it surely did, seeing the shrouded form upon its bier in the side chapel, it was swiftly wiped away. Voices gave a response to the priest's enquiries steadily, without a hint of quailing. Smiles took a deal of effort, but they were there, all the same, welcoming the babe as a member of God's flock, a new soul to be loved and cherished. Naught was permitted to spoil the joy of tiny Richard's special moment, even if he would have no memory of it. Cousin

Joan cradled him as if he was her own child which, hopefully, she would have one day. Adam was a proud godfather indeed, making a far better show of introducing the babe to the congregation than I could have done, being yet afeared of dropping him. Father John Haughton himself stood as the required second godfather, *in lieu* of my brother Jude, back in London: a concession I earnestly desired that the priest had granted. It pleased me greatly, but I was unsure that Emily would likewise agree. I suspected she would have much to say against my choice of the second godfather when I dared to inform her – some other day.

With the christening concluded, Cousin Joan carried the babe back home in triumph, accompanied by the women of Foxley, even some of those from the Upper End. They would share bread and ale at our cottage, gossip and laugh and, in this instance, probably console one another. There was also a funeral repast to organise for the morrow. At this time of year, the burial could not be delayed.

As was the tradition, the men – Nether Enders at least – retired to Uncle Harry Oakenshaw's tavern to wet the babe's head a second time with ale. Man's equivalent of God's holy water used earlier during the baptism, I suppose. But it didn't feel right. The tavern had an emptiness that had naught to do with the number of customers for they were numerous indeed. Rather, the lack of my cousin's vast height and breadth of shoulder, his hearty laugh: that made the alehouse seem half empty and the company was doleful and too quiet. No bawdy songs were sung; not a single lewd jest told. No one laughed. We sipped our ale thoughtfully and Uncle Oakenshaw's dour expression did not help raise anyone's spirits.

'At least there won't be any trouble this eve,' he said, setting down another jug full of ale in front of Adam, Cousin John and me. An unexpected benevolence which surprised us all since we hadn't ordered it and he asked for no coin.

Steward Bayard came clumping in through the tavern doorway and, espying us, came and sat at our table, bellowing at

Harry Oakenshaw to bring another cup. Having helped himself to our ale, he got comfortable, adjusting the leather belt over his paunch and loosening his furred robe, revealing the inevitable damp sweat stains on the doublet beneath. Why he wore such clothes at midsummer was baffling.

''Tis as well I've found you,' he said, frowning at us from beneath his bushy grey brows. 'I have questions about this afternoon.'

'Not now, Bayard,' Adam told him. 'Can you not see? This be a welcome to Seb's little lad to celebrate his christening – from which you absented yourself. An omission that did not go unremarked upon in church.'

'This cannot wait. Luke Forester was an oaf and a cuckolding lout, but he deserves justice even so.'

'Trying to win friends as ever, Bayard?' Adam's tone was caustic. 'Luke was a respected man of the village and don't you dare say otherwise, 'less you want a broken nose.'

'Nay, Adam,' I said, speaking calmly as I might, 'Cousin Bayard be correct. Luke's killer must pay for his crime and the sooner we find him out, the better. A murderer should not go unpunished. Back in London, my brother, Jude, and I have aided the coroner and sheriffs on occasion to solve such heinous crimes. Poisonings, stabbings, arson – we have had some few successes.'

'How so? How can you name the felon unless he confesses?' Bayard gave me a quizzical look, as though he wanted to believe me but found my story unlikely.

'Each case was different, but so often a murderer leaves behind a clue.'

'Well, not this time. The victim was slashed by a sword,' Bayard said, making a sideways cutting action with his hand. 'Whose sword, we know not. Few men on the manor even own or could lay a hand to such a weapon. And no one's seen any strangers of late who might bear one. Unless you know otherwise – which is what I have to ask.'

51

'Cousin Luke did not die by the sword,' I said. 'But by a more humble weapon. Did you not see how the gashes went around his body, not straight across? The deed was done with a long curving blade. He was slain with a scythe.'

'By the Dear Christ, Seb!' Adam gasped. 'Be you certain of this?'

'It was clear enough to see.' Except that no one else had looked so close as I. They saw a dying or dead man and that was more than enough, I realised.

'Then that presents a vast problem, doesn't it?' Bayard said, sounding almost pleased. 'Since everyone was thus armed – including you,' he said, poking my chest with a pudgy finger, 'How do we tell who did it, eh? You tell me how, Master Londoner, with your know-it-all ways. This is an unsolvable crime, even for you, is it not? Or are you the guilty party, perhaps? Did he make a green-gown of that pretty wife of yours, too?'

Adam's fist flew across the table and the steward fell backwards off his stool afore I was even aware.

'Do not dare insult Sebastian and Emily with your filthy accusations,' Adam roared. 'You are a more likely felon. I saw you with a scythe in your hand also and you had grievances against Luke as Seb did not. We all know Luke had a fancy for your wife, Eleanor, in her younger days.'

That surprised me indeed, but of course, there must be much I did not know about what went on in the village afore I came. I pulled Adam back down onto the bench beside me.

'Softly, Adam. No need for this.' I poured him more ale to cool his humours.

'Behave yourselves in my tavern,' Uncle Oakenshaw growled, coming over to drag Bayard to his feet and right the stool. 'I've had enough broken furniture of late and no man's paid for a stick of it so far.'

'I apologise, uncle,' I said. 'We are all of us out of humour this eve. I will recompense you on the morrow if you remind me then.'

'Aye, well. Maybe so,' he muttered and stomped back behind his serving board.

Bayard sat, dabbing at his bloody nose. The look in his eye declared his difficulty in restraining himself from taking revenge upon Adam. They were like two bristling tomcats confined in a box.

Cousin John looked on, wearily shaking his head, having said little throughout the evening but 'aye' or 'nay' and 'thanking you'. He was grieving and our conversation had distressed him.

'I believe there may be a means of determining who robbed Cousin Luke of his life,' I said. 'But that will be a matter for the morrow, when we gather in the field to finish the haymaking. For now, I will see Cousin John home to his bed. Come, John. Finish your ale. We all are weary.'

By the time I reached home, the women had gone, except for that benevolent soul, Cousin Joan, who had stayed to aid Em in washing up the borrowed cups and platters and folding away the linen tablecloths, kindly lent for the christening supper. Gawain assisted by eating the best of the fallen crumbs afore Cousin Joan swept the floor. The long summer twilight was fading and I bade Joan to make her way to the Foresters' cottage afore the light was gone for it was the dark of the moon this night.

Thinking I should show willing, I lighted a taper and went to look upon my son in his cradle. Was it not the way that children were supposed to have some likeness to their parents? The hairless, toothless, plump-cheeked bundle bore not the least similarity of feature to either of us that I could see. Was it any wonder I felt little attachment to him, other than the weight of responsibility? Was something amiss with me that paternal love seemed utterly lacking in my heart? In truth, my uppermost sentiment was fear. Fear that I would fail him in the future, drop him or cause him harm even when I did not intend it.

I could recall every word of my father's letter to me, penned when he knew he had not long to live, telling how he had damaged me in a fit of temper, crippling me for years with shoulder and hip displaced. His kindness towards me thereafter had not mended the injuries until a miracle had come to pass, long after my father died. I believe now that my ruined body was *his* punishment from God, not mine, such that the Almighty granted me a miraculous recovery when my father was no more and I was so sore in need. Was that why this tiny child affrighted me? Aye, the fear that I would repeat my parent's awful sin. But I was not a man of anger and ill-temper, was I? I prayed that I should learn to love him.

Chapter 4

Thursday, the eighteenth day of June

THE NEXT morn, as the sun rose beyond the manor house, Steward Bayard was at our door, even so early. I was still pulling on my stout working boots. They had previously belonged to Adam's brother, Noah – may the Lord God grant him peace and bless his soul.

'You told me last eve that you know a means of determining who killed Luke Forester,' he said without giving any greeting. 'There is no reason to delay. I want this matter dealt with now. I have to have the haymaking done whilst the weather holds fair and then the manor prepared for the arrival of the bridal party next week. So much to do. Come, get yourself out to the field.'

'You be an impatient fellow, Cousin Bayard,' I complained. 'I haven't broken my fast as yet, nor said my prayers for the day.'

At that moment, the babe began to wail, wanting to break his fast also, no doubt. It seemed reason enough to leave so I murmured a Paternoster and an Ave Maria, crossed myself, took a hasty swig of ale, snatched up a piece of bread in one hand and a lump of cheese in the other, called to Gawain and bade Em farewell. She would be wholly concerned with the babe and not miss me until dinnertime.

'How will you get a confession out of the guilty man?' Steward Bayard enquired as we walked toward the half-cut hayfield.

I had no intention of explaining my means to him. There was no certainty that what I had in mind would even work. Gawain loped along, often plunging his nose in among the hedgerow flowers and grasses, scenting the invisible trails left by the creatures of the night. It was his actions of yesterday which had given me the possible solution; a means to identify the felon. That and the flies.

We stood in the field, waiting. Bayard had dragged me here right early, but the rest of the villagers were in no such hurry. Singly, in pairs and small groups, the tardy labourers arrived, carrying their scythes over their shoulders and their water bottles strapped to their belts. All were wearing hats to keep off the sun except for me. Adam arrived with his father, Thomas, my half-brother – a man of few words, indeed. Uncle Harry Oakenshaw came with Cousin John and Nicholas Rudd, but there was no sign of the other Rudds, nor the Persloes and the Meades from the Upper End. Bayard was muttering curses under his breath at the delay.

I watched them all, realising with a shiver that one among them was a vicious killer and I was here to unmask him. Who was it? It might be someone to whom I felt close; a relative maybe; a neighbour almost certainly. I prayed it would be someone from the Upper End but feared it was unlikely, unless Luke's death had been purely by mischance and not intended.

At last, the entire company of labourers was assembled and an unhappy crowd it was.

'Why so early, Bayard?' Adam asked the question on all their lips. ''Tis not as though it looks likely to rain.'

Bayard ignored him but turned to me.

'How do we do this? How should we go about it?'

'Tell them all to lay their scythes in a row in full sun upon the cut grass,' I said.

'Then what?'

'Then we wait and watch.'

'There's no time to waste on such foolishness.'

'You want to know who killed Luke, do you not?'

'Aye, of course.'

'Then proceed as I say... and put your scythe along with the others.'

'Mine? I don't have one.'

'The one you gave me to use yesterday. There must be no exceptions if this is to be a fair test.'

'Test? How so?'

'You will see, as shall we all.'

In all, there were thirty-five scythes lined up – thirty-six with the one Steward Bayard had forced me to make use of so unskilfully. I turned to the labourers. Adam came towards me, but I waved him back to his place. I could not have anybody thinking I favoured one above the others or, worse yet, that I had colluded with those I loved best.

'Yesterday,' I said, raising my voice such that all might hear, 'It was explained to me that every man has his own scythe, weighted and balanced to suit his build and way of handling. Is that the truth of it?'

Heads nodded. A few said 'aye'.

'Is that the truth of it?' I repeated. They agreed it was. 'And each scythe be marked with the sign of its owner. Is that true also?' That too was agreed, but I noted a few shuffled their feet, scratched at fleas or hitched up their breeches. They were becoming nervous. 'You be aware, every one of you, that Luke Forester was slain yesterday, here in the woodland behind us. But some among you may not know that he was killed with a scythe.'

Some gasped at my revelation. Others muttered and mumbled. All wondered at what I was about.

'One of these scythes is the murder weapon and I shall find it out and know its owner for the man who killed Luke Forester.'

With Steward Bayard at my right hand and Gawain at my left, I walked slowly along the line of implements. All had been cleaned and sharpened, as I expected, but they were not so scoured that a fine nose could no longer scent the odour of blood, trapped betwixt the wooden handle and the blade. It had been my fear that the felon might have been zealous in his cleaning, but it seemed that having wiped away any visible blood, that was deemed sufficient. As I hoped, Gawain discovered one particular scythe that took his interest, but even he proved a late-comer to the task for the flies had found it out already, swarming around the blade. I wondered whose it was. My suspicion, following the debâcle at the tavern upon the eve afore last, was that it might be Nick Parfitt's.

'This be the murderous blade!' I cried. Steward Bayard bent down to examine it more closely. Dried blood was evident upon the handle even to our human sense of sight, as was the mark of ownership scratched into the wood. I did not know for certain whose it was, but I might hazard a guess: an oak leaf on an ale tun.

'Seize Harry Oakenshaw!' the steward yelled. 'Hold the devil.'

After a moment or two of hesitation at the shock of it, many hands made a grab for the tavern-keeper as he attempted to hobble away. He could not escape and his curses served for naught.

I realised then that Cousin Luke, in his last precious instants of life, told me who had slain him. Had he not chosen an oak leaf purposely from all the woodland litter around him and pressed it into my hand? I still had it back at the cottage somewhere, thinking to preserve it as a keepsake of my cousin, but it was so much more than that: a message from a dead man. I harboured no doubts now that we had the miscreant and no other.

'Why, uncle?' I asked him.

'Why else? Because he was an insult to the Lord God; a filthy fornicator. He betrayed my Cecily, his loving and dutiful wife. Having worn her to the bone, he takes his pleasure wherever he pleases, whether other men's wives or unsullied maidens. His kind deserves to die without any chance of confession and absolution; to go straight to the torments of Hell.'

'And what of you, Oakenshaw; a bloody murderer?' the steward demanded. 'You'll be joining him there.'

'I be ready and willing to do so. My reward shall be twofold: to watch him suffering in hellfire and to know I've spared my daughter yet more heartache, humiliation and misery as his wife.'

'You think her widowhood with five children to feed and no man to win their bread will be easier? You be a fool if you do.' Adam was shaking his head in puzzlement. 'And who'll run the tavern now, eh?'

The lark was singing his carol once more, high in the vault of Heaven. I was thus reminded how little a man's passing – even one of such presence as Cousin Luke – affected the world. Nature continued, wonderful and carefree, no matter what heartache men suffered. And there was Gawain, gambolling like a spring lamb up The Street, towards the church. Naught daunted his delight in living either. He buried his nose in a clump of daisies, sneezing on their pollen and disturbing a bumble bee.

'Come, Gawain, can you not be a little more solemn this day?' I chided him.

He sneezed again, relieving himself upon a stand of cow parsley afore chasing after a white butterfly in a cloud of dust, so it seemed he could not.

Everyone else was still at work in the hayfield, but I would return to my abandoned mural. I was displeased at the remembrance of the wasted azurite pigment of yesterday.

Despite the loss of the fine blue pigment that had to be discarded, having turned to the stone from which it had come in the bottom of the pot, I was soon engrossed in my painting of the mural. Gawain was dozing in a shaft of lucent sunlight that showed every mote of dust on his silky coat. He flicked an ear and flexed a paw as he dreamed. Uncle Harry Oakenshaw would not be disturbing us in order to make his prayers since he was now kept under guard over at the manor house, awaiting the arrival of the coroner from Norwich to perform his inquest. I could but hope he would come this day for – though I would never speak ill of the dead – there was no denying that Cousin Luke's sorry remains were beginning to add a faint but unsavoury odour to the air, even within the cool of the church. Steward Bayard had informed me in his most peremptory tone that I would be required to give testimony at the inquest to be held at the manor as soon as convenient for the coroner. Therefore, I needs must get on with my painting for fear of further interruptions.

Being now somewhat short of blue pigments, I determined that it should not go amiss if I eked out the remaining azurite with a little verdigris – a greenish tint to the highlights of the folds in the angels' robes would not be detrimental to the overall effect, I thought. In truth, the addition created a pleasing turquoise colour that I applied to the image with a steady hand in long downward strokes, as to give the illusion of folded blue-green silk catching the light. Most limners frown upon the mixing of pigments of differing hues, claiming that it denigrates their purity. They prefer to apply a single colour and then over-paint it with a second to create a third tone, yet the colours cannot fully merge because the first is dry when the second is applied. This was the method my master, Richard Collop, had taught me and to which I have always adhered. Have I discovered a new way of mixing two pigments whilst they be wet to create a novel colour indeed? When I have leisure enough and pigments to spare, I shall experiment with the possibilities of this.

My musings were ended by the arrival of Adam from the manor house, come to summon me to attend the inquest. The coroner had ridden from Norwich and wanted his duties done afore supper, so all was in haste. Fortunately, I had just completed painting the angelic attire, so no pigments would be wasted this time. I rinsed out the brush and climbed down from my high perch with due care.

'Will the coroner not be coming here, to the church, to view the, er, body?' I asked Adam, finding it hard to refer to my cousin thus.

He shrugged.

'I'm not the man to ask, am I now? Who knows what the fellow may decide. I was told to fetch the first-finder – you – and you're to bring the dog also since he be a first-finder of a sort too.'

'As were you,' I reminded him as I closed the great door of the church and returned the key to its box in the porch.

'Aye, and I've said my piece already, explaining why and how we searched for Luke. Now the coroner would hear your version of events.'

'Which will be the same as yours, if we both speak true. You didn't embellish the facts, did you, Adam? Else our tales will not tally and it will look bad for us.'

'Nay.' He shook his head. 'But I did omit a few things, somewhat. Naught of significance, I swear.'

'Oh? You best tell me what you left unsaid.'

'I never told them about throwing up when I saw it. And I didn't mention the fight. After all, that might make it seem that any number of us had a grudge against him.'

I sighed.

'You should have mentioned that at least, Adam, for someone is certain to speak of it and then the coroner will have cause to wonder why you did not.'

'I never thought of that. Oh, Seb, I know naught about the doings of the law. Have I caused difficulties for us, do you suppose?' Adam kicked at the dust as we turned along Manor Lane. 'Shall I be in trouble?'

'Did the coroner enquire directly of you, concerning whether you and Luke were forever amicable, on the best of terms?'

'I don't recall that he did. I think not, but I was flustered. I've ne'er been questioned afore, and my mind was all in confusion.'

'Then, if the matter arises, that is what you must say: that you were confused by the questioning and forgot to mention what occurred in the tavern, not realising it might be relevant.'

'They'll take me for a lackwit in that case. Otherwise, how could a fight, from which cause I still bear a split lip and bruises aplenty, have slipped my memory so soon?'

'Cannot be helped now, Adam,' I said, squeezing his shoulder. 'I be sure all will be well. Fear not. 'Twas a simple error to make.'

Adam and I crossed the wooden bridge over the murky waters of the moat and entered beneath the gatehouse. It must once have been imposing, but now the portcullis looked to be riveted together with rust and would most likely never serve its purpose again. Weeds sprouted amidst the cobbles of the courtyard and at the base of the buildings surrounding it upon three sides, though they had been trampled by recent activity. Ivy draped the walls and nettles thrived in sunlit corners. The manor did not appear to be well maintained and I wondered that a bridal party should choose to come here in the near future. The reasons for Steward Bayard's sudden panic to have the place set to rights were plainly evident. Perhaps its years of neglect were my cousin's failure and the earl was expecting to return to a fine, well-ordered residence, in which case he would be sorely disappointed. Even the few stone steps into the great hall were chipped and a dandelion plant boldly thrust its golden flowers through a cracked paving slab.

Within, the great hall looked well enough, if old-fashioned and dowdy compared to the luxuries and finest appointments of Crosby Place, the Duke of Gloucester's house in London. I could speak with some authority on this having spent time there of late, painting the duke's portrait, but Adam nudged me, told me to hold my tongue and not boast about such things.

I accepted my reprimand humbly. He was right: Foxley had no interest in the excesses of London's grandeur. The hall was crowded. It seemed almost the entire village was present. Only my Emily was missing that I could name and Uncle Harry Oakenshaw who must be under lock and key somewhere.

As soon as he saw us, Steward Bayard beckoned me towards the dais, giving Gawain a wary look as the dog followed me.

'Tardy as ever, Londoner,' he complained. 'Why is it I always have to send for you or drag you out myself, eh?'

'Am I supposed to foresee the future then, cousin, to know without being informed when my attendance will be required? As of this morn, the coroner's arrival this day was still uncertain, was it not?'

'Don't be impertinent, lickspittle, I warn you.' We approached the dais where a man sprawled in a cushioned chair, flanked by clerks on either hand. His attire looked to have been costly once but was now shabby and shrouded in the dust of travel. He wore his years even less well. Bald of head and flabby of girth, his eyes were shadowed and his brow creased. The coroner seemed weary and sour humoured. Steward Bayard announced me by name.

'Sebastian Armitage,' the coroner growled. 'First-finder and brother of the other finder, Adam Armitage. What have you to say for yourself? Baldwin: put him under oath then note down his replies.' He waved at one of the clerks.

'Good day, Sir Coroner,' I said, removing my cap and bowing my head. My gesture of courtesy was ignored.

'Take this Gospel book in your hand,' the clerk told me, offering a well-worn volume. 'Now, do you swear upon your oath, as you shall make answer on Judgement Day, to speak the truth, the entire truth and naught else but the truth, in the name of the Blessed Trinity?'

'I do so swear,' I said clearly, handing back the book. 'But I would correct the court. Adam Armitage is not my brother but rather the son of my elder half-brother.'

'No matter. I care not if he be your bloody mother-by-marriage which in these devil's dens of incest and inter-relatedness is all too likely.' The coroner drained his cup and held it out to be refilled. The second clerk obliged. 'Tell the court what came to pass yester afternoon when you found the corpse and be swift about it. You miserable bumpkins bore me so.'

'Aye, sir. It was after the dinner hour of rest, as work was about to begin again in the hayfield, we realised my cousin, Luke Forester, was no longer there among the labourers and a man such as he be hard to overlook.'

'Why is that?' the coroner demanded.

'For why he stands a head taller than any other and as broad again as any man in Foxley,' I explained.

The coroner nodded at me to continue.

'There is a small area of woodland beside the western end of the field and some of the men had sought shade beneath the trees there. When Luke failed to answer our calls, we went into the copse to search for him, thinking he might be...' I considered my words with care, 'Taking a nap after the meal.'

'Taking a piss or having a quick fuck more likely,' someone called out from the assembled villagers. A ripple of laughter passed through the court, like a breeze bestirring a cornfield. The coroner thumped the arm of his chair with the hilt of his knife to restore order.

'Get on with it, Armitage.' I realised the coroner meant me.

'In short, sir, my dog it was that found Luke Forester lying beneath a tree.'

'Your dog was first-finder of the corpse?'

'Not exactly, sir. When my dog found him, my cousin was yet alive, if only just...' A loud murmur, like a beehive disturbed, spread through the assembly.

'The other first-finder said naught of the man still breathing when you discovered him. Why would that be?'

'P-perhaps Adam did not look so closely as I did,' I stammered. 'H-he may not have realised Luke was not dead.'

Oh, no. Our versions of the events did not agree. This was a bad thing indeed. It never occurred to me that I alone knew my cousin still lived for a few moments, time enough to give me the oak leaf afore he died in my arms. I had told no one of this; not even Adam, but I thought he knew – wrongly, so it turned out. Or was it another of his omissions?

The coroner nodded and sighed.

'No matter,' he said, mumbling into his beard. 'Steward Bayard has described how you determined who had killed this fellow, er, Forester. I would now hear your tale – briefly. And it had better agree with his or you'll be in trouble.'

This was a worry, indeed. I had not heard the Steward's testimony so how might I know if our stories tallied. All I could do was tell the truth and trust that he had done likewise. I described to the court how I had every man's scythe laid out in full view to await my dog's searching nose to discover any traces of blood but, in the event, the black gathering of flies had marked the offending blade afore ever my dog drew close.

'And why were you convinced in the first instance that a scythe had been the instrument of death?' the coroner asked.

'By the shape of the wounds, sir, which curved across and around t-the body.' I breathed deeply to steady myself.

'And you have some expertise in such matters, no doubt.' He sniggered and others joined him. Clearly, he meant it as a jest, so my answer surprised him.

'I do, sir. I have, upon occasion, assisted the deputy coroner and sheriffs in London by drawing corpses that cannot be named at the time. The hope is that relatives or friends may be found to identify them from my drawings even after the corpse has been buried. In this capacity, I have seen wounds and injuries of many kinds and it has been known for my sketches to assist also in discovering the kind of weapon used.'

'And you have seen the wounds caused by a scythe on one of these occasions?'

'No, sir, but I have seen the injury caused by the blade of a sickle which is smaller but likewise curved.'

'I know how a sickle looks. So murder was done by means of a scythe. You and Steward Bayard agree on that. How much is the scythe in question worth?'

This was the usual way of a coroner's court: the value of the weapon most often reflected the wealth of the owner; a bejewelled dagger worth more than a bone-handled knife. Thus any fines imposed upon the miscreant could be based on the size of his purse. I was told to step down and one of the Persloes from the Upper End – Gilbert, I believe it was, though the family resemblance among them was so marked, I always had trouble knowing them apart – was called forward. Gilbert was indeed named and instructed to swear the oath. Being the village blacksmith, he would understand the quality and likely value of any blade. He made much of his moment of fame with a good deal of frowning, considering and clearing of his throat before announcing that the blade was worth nine pence three farthings by his reckoning. The handle, being somewhat split from lack of proper care of the wood was worth two pence and the lead bands used to weight it were valued at a penny ha'penny. All together, he announced, with the cost of labour to make another like it, the scythe was worth one shilling and two pence farthing.

'Note that down, Baldwin,' the coroner instructed, unnecessarily, since the clerk had been scribbling furiously throughout Gilbert's deliberation and final pronouncement. 'Coin or goods to that value to be taken as an amercement for King Edward from the owner of the scythe. Whose is it?'

'Henry Oakenshaw's, the tavern-keeper,' Steward Bayard said, unable to entirely conceal the pleasure he felt. The Armitages made no secret of their dislike for their matriarch's second marriage to an Oakenshaw. Apart from their enjoyment of Oakenshaw ale, that is. There would be no more of that now.

The coroner chewed his lip, thinking. 'And there can be no doubt that Henry Oakenshaw used his own scythe as the murder weapon? No other could have taken it up, knowing Oakenshaw would be accused in his stead?'

The murmuring grew as the court considered the possibility. I reappraised my opinion of the Norwich coroner: a wily fellow indeed. I stepped forward.

'Sir Coroner, forgive my interruption, but I do have evidence of a sort, if the court allows?'

He raised his hand to give assent.

I took from my purse a folded square of parchment. I opened it to reveal a leaf. It was becoming fragile, drying and crisping, fading to the pale colour of last year's straw but that made the blood stains upon it stand out more blatantly.

'My cousin, Luke Forester, pressed this single leaf into my hand as he lay dying, insisting I took it even as he drew his last breath. He could not speak, but he chose this one leaf from the litter around him, grabbing a handful then letting all others but this fall from his bloody grasp. I be certain it was his way of telling me who had slain him. 'Tis an oak leaf.'

The coroner took it from me, holding it to the light from the dusty windows.

'This could be any of ten thousand such leaves in the woodlands. You could have picked it up at any time, from anywhere,' he said.

'It is stained with blood, now dried but not from so long ago, sir.'

'That might be any man's blood. Or the blood of a pig or sheep or some other beast.'

''Tis true,' I admitted, 'And impossible to prove, I know, but I have not forgotten that I pledged my oath to speak truly less than an hour since, sir. Upon the peril of my soul, I declare that Luke Forester gave this into my hand as he died. If I be assuming, wrongly, that with an oak leaf he was thus naming his killer, then I beg pardon of the Lord God, this court and the man I have taken to be the felon in this case.'

After considerable thought, the coroner nodded and dismissed me.

'Enter the leaf as evidence in the court roll, Baldwin,' he instructed. 'Inquest is ended. Henry Oakenshaw stands accused of murder, of causing Luke Forester to die by means other than his rightful death. He is to be taken to Norwich to stand trial at the next sessions. Court is adjourned.'

'I should go to Old Mother Oakenshaw's place,' I told Adam as we were walking back from the manor. 'I promised to affix a new sheet of parchment in her window days ago, but now I cannot think how to talk to her, what to say after such events. Besides, I am the one who has identified her son as a murderer. She will probably sooner spit upon my shadow than let me cross her threshold. What am I to do?'

'Leave it a while. The weather is yet fair. As soon as it rains and she finds puddles 'neath the window, she will be happy to see you.' He put his arm about my shoulders. ''Tis hardly your fault that her son is a bad lot. You saw justice done is all.'

'I know, but I feel uncomfortable about it. If only some other could have been guilty instead of our own uncle. It taints us all.'

'We have no Oakenshaw blood in our veins, Seb. We're Armitages. That makes us free of his taint. Fear not.'

'But I promised our grandmother that I would mend her window. I always try to keep my word.'

'You make a rod to beat your own back,' Adam said with a sigh. 'If your conscience pricks you so you feel obliged to mend something, you can come to the manor. Bayard will be frantic at this delay for the inquest. You've seen the state of the place; how much work is required to set it to rights in less than a se'en-night. Of course, 'tis his own fault. If he had maintained it as a steward should and not let it nigh crumble about his ears from neglect, it would be in good order to receive its lord.'

We turned in at the house. I could see Em through the open door: babe in one hand, ladle in the other, stirring the pottage for dinner.

'Are you instructed to sweep bedchambers, air linen and dust cobwebs, then?' I asked him.

'Most certainly not. I've been wearing my fingers to the bone, writing letters, organising the purchase of fine foodstuffs and wine from Norwich, oats for the extra horses, not to mention materials for repairing the place. I tell you, Seb, I even had to order...'

'Are you two going to wash your hands and eat or stand there, chewing the cud like a yoke of oxen all day?' Emily said, putting the babe into his cradle. He snuffled and hiccoughed a few times afore lying quiet, sleeping.

We obeyed and made use of the laver bowl. Once seated at the board, I said a prayer of thanksgiving for our good dinner then we set about the pottage. The peas were freshly picked from our garden plot and so green and sweet we all enjoyed it. Alongside the pottage, Em had fried the emptied peapods in butter and sprinkled them with parsley. It was a fine dinner. As we finished with wild strawberries in a creamed sauce – a king's delicacy indeed – I asked Adam to tell us more about the preparations up at the manor.

'Well, they won't be eating any better than this, I can tell you,' he said, patting his belly. 'That was excellent, Em. But I've had to order enough pepper, saffron, ginger and sugar to feed an army for a year, I swear.'

'An army wouldn't get such luxuries,' Em told him.

'Well, no, but you take my meaning: such extravagance! The earl is sending his own cooks too, which be as well since none of us would know what to do with spices.'

'I could tell you,' Em said. 'I know many receipts that use them. Is that not so, Seb?'

'Aye. We used a good deal of saffron afore we left London. Em had a great longing for it when she was first with child.'

'And you still begrudge it!'

'I do not, my sweet.' I could tell by my wife's expression that this exchange might become a quarrel, so I turned to Adam. 'When are these people expected and who will be coming?' I took up my dinner knife anew, wiped it clean on a napkin and used it to trim my fingernails that were growing overlong.

'Monday or Tuesday next. There'll be the Earl of Kent, Edmund Grey, of course, and both his sons, Anthony and George, since they are the bridegrooms.'

Those two names: 'Anthony and George' sent a shiver up my spine in memory of recent times back in London. The death of George, Duke of Clarence, at the hands of Queen Elizabeth Woodville and her brother Anthony, Earl Rivers, was the reason Em and I had fled the city in haste, discovering my life was in danger from their scheming. Somewhat distracted by my unquiet thoughts, it seemed I misheard what Adam said next.

'And the brides' family – they both being sisters to the queen – with Anthony Woodville to oversee the ceremonies, he being godfather to his namesake, Anthony Grey.'

My knife clattered to the floor; my blood ran cold in my veins and I became dizzy, seeing Adam's face blur and waver in my sight.

'Oh, Seb. What shall we do?' Em asked, her voice as shaky as I felt. 'We dare not stay here. Suppose they hear your name?'

'What be amiss? You both look as though the Devil has walked through the door.'

'He has. Dear Lord, save us. Adam, this is the worst that might come to pass for us.' I reached for my ale cup, spilling it as I attempted to refill it from the jug. Adam obliged me and gave the drink into my hand.

'Tell me.'

Thus I explained to him how the Woodvilles had tried more than once to have me slain, fearing that I knew too much concerning Clarence's death at the Tower of London and mayhap other matters besides. They were correct in thinking so, but I had no intention of ever revealing all that I knew. I had told Richard, Duke of Gloucester, the circumstances surrounding the death of his brother, the possibility of the Woodvilles' involvement but only the facts and not supposition. Richard could unravel the truth for himself, if he wished but, even to him I never repeated what Clarence had told me of the queen's secret reason why he had to die. I did not tell Adam the full story either. None knew of it, but me and it was knowledge too terrible to share. However, I made certain Adam was fully aware that Foxley now, of a sudden, was no longer a safe refuge for Em and me.

He puffed out a breath.

''Tis quite a story, Seb. I never realised your life was in peril. There was I, thinking you had fallen into debt or been caught out in some underhanded shady dealings. They really did try to kill you? I can scarce believe it.'

'I couldn't believe it myself, but by the third attempt, when I was shot with an arrow in broad daylight in the midst of the city street as folk were leaving High Mass, I was convinced at last. We had little choice then but to leave London and we came here, thinking we would be safe so far from the king's court. Yet it seems we are mistaken: trouble has followed us even to remotest Norfolk.'

'We're not exactly distant Outremer, Seb,' Adam said, pulling a face at my description of his home, 'But I see your point. The Woodvilles have a long reach, it seems.'

That night, I knew I should not be able to sleep for worrying. Em was unhappy too, fearful of the near future and even the babe was fretful as if he sensed our unease. So, not bothered about seeking my restless bed, I went outside our door, towards The Street, looking across the meadows at the vast expanse of sky. I knew for as long as I lived, I should never forget the Norfolk skies. This moonless night was an endless swathe of blackest velvet spangled with stars beyond the wit of man to count, diamond lights strewn at the Creator's whim for our delight. I breathed the scents of summer, always more definite after the sun set: the fragrance of wild woodbine drew moths, fluttering, ghostly and colourless in the starlight. The perfume of lavender, sweet cicely and the new-cut hay still lay heavy in the warm, soft airs. I called to Em, and she joined me.

'Is the babe settled?' I asked, folding my arms about her from behind. She leant back against my chest, her unbound hair soft upon my cheek.

'Aye, Dickon is sleeping, for the moment, at least.'

'Look at the sky, Em. Do its beauty and grandeur not make our troubles seem of far lesser consequence? Does such magnificence not reflect the wonder and power of the Almighty? Does it not take your breath away?'

'Aye, 'tis beautiful, I grant, but so cold and distant. To me, it makes God seem so far removed from us. Sometimes, I don't think He loves mankind any longer. Arranging stars must give Him more pleasure.'

'Oh, Em, what a sorrowful thing to say. Of course God loves us: He sent his Son to redeem us all. You know that.'

'Do I?'

'He has blessed us with a fine babe.'

'I suppose so.'

I turned Em to face me and kissed her lips.

'He has given me you as my wife,' I whispered. 'If the Lord never grants me another boon, I shall not be downhearted for what man has a right to expect more when his heart's desire has been fulfilled? You are my treasure, my soulmate, Em. I be satisfied with that.'

'Truly?'

'Aye. Truly, indeed.'

Chapter 5

Friday, the nineteenth day of June

'I'M COMING with you to London,' Adam said.

I was up on the scaffold planks, painting the rocky pathway the damned must tread towards the gaping mouth of Hell. I was determined to complete the mural afore we had to leave the village.

'Why in God's holy name would you do that, Adam? Your life be here in Foxley.'

He shrugged.

'There's naught but a lifetime of being at Bayard's beck and call. Would you want that?'

'But what of your parents? They need you.'

'Need me? They barely deign to notice my existence since Noah died. He was the favourite and they blame me that he died rather than me.'

'You could go back to Norwich, then, work as a scrivener there, become a master of the craft.'

'Nay. My father couldn't afford the premium for me to do any better than be a journeyman when my 'prentiship was done. I'll never be a master stationer there, but in London, who knows what fortunes are to be made?'

I laughed.

'You think the streets be paved with gold, no doubt? I warn

you, Adam, most of the streets be paved with mud, ordure and rubbish, like other towns I saw upon my journey here and worse than most. The stink will affright you indeed.'

'Norwich hardly smelled of flower garlands; I'll get used to it – if you'll have me? I could work as your journeyman until I find a master of my own. You may recommend me to your fellow stationers: you know my work is of a high standard.'

'What of your other relatives and friends? All the Foresters will miss you so and at this, their time of loss, your going too will make matters worse yet.'

'I'll come with you all the same. You'll need my aid upon the journey, what with Em still recovering and a new babe to tend to. An extra pair of hands will be an asset to you. And I can pay my way: I have coin saved. I won't add to your burden.'

'But, Adam...' I washed out my brush and began to climb down the ladder.

'Don't make me plead with you, Seb. I've been considering leaving ever since Noah passed. And now Luke's gone, there is naught here for me any longer and London seems as good a place as any to begin anew. Besides, to speak true, you are more of a brother to me now, sent by God's own kindness to save me from despair without Noah. You and Em are more like close family.' He paused and moved closer. 'I love you, Seb.'

His speech had brought tears to my eyes and a constriction to my throat. Words would not come, so I drew him into my embrace. We stood thus until I recovered my voice.

'You will be more than welcome, Adam, you know that.' I stood back a little, turning to practical matters. 'We must be packed up and prepared to leave first thing Monday morn else I fear encountering the Woodvilles upon the road.'

'Would they recognise you?'

'Not Earl Anthony himself, for we have never met, but it was his servants or hirelings who came after me. Who can say whether any of them may be numbered in his entourage? I would be a fool to take the risk.'

'Will you be any safer in London than you were before?'
Adam asked. It was a wise question but one I couldn't answer
with any certainty.

'I know not. Months have passed; circumstances change. If
we bide quietly and draw no attention to ourselves, hopefully,
we may go unremarked among the citizens as once was the case.
Lord Richard will not be there, such that his patronage will call
me to the notice of folk in high places. That be the best we may
do: conceal ourselves in a crowd.'

That eve, after vespers, Cousin Luke was buried in the
churchyard among his ancestors. Afterwards, we menfolk all
went to the Foresters' cottage. It might have been more usual
to go to the tavern and leave the women to grieve at home, but
since the alehouse was the abode of Luke's killer, we were not of
a mind to go there. Instead, the women went to our cottage so
that Em could share the solemn occasion. Thank the Virgin, Em
shall be churched afore High Mass on Sunday and may then be
seen beyond our gate. 'Tis somewhat a hurried churching but it
cannot be otherwise since we must be upon our journey the day
after. Steward Bayard be wondering at our sudden decision, as
are others in the village, but I dare not tell the true reason to any
but Father John Haughton and Aunt Marjorie who alone knew
why first we came here. Even to them, the name of 'Woodville'
has never been mentioned, only that my requirement for a safe
haven away from London be no longer the case and we wish
to go home. This last is true for Em: she longs to see her father
and brother, Dame Ellen and her friends again, to hear of my
brother's marriage to Rose – that should have occurred at Easter
– and to show off our babe. I want to see Jude, most certainly,
but I have been happy here and will miss my new-found family.
Also, I be wondering how Jude will take to meeting Adam, our
nephew who be more like a brother to me. Jude has never been
an easy fellow to gauge his humour. Might he feel jealousy

towards Adam? Or feel that I have attempted to place my brotherly affections elsewhere? Or begrudge him a position in our home and workshop? Or will he take a great liking to Adam straightway, as I did? I pray it may be so.

Author's Notes

The manor of Foxley village in Norfolk was one of numerous estates owned by Edmund Grey, Earl of Kent, in the late fifteenth century. As in the story, both the earl's sons, Anthony and George, did marry sisters of Queen Elizabeth Woodville, Eleanor and Anne, although I was unable to find dates for either wedding so felt free to arrange a double event at the worst time possible from our hero's point of view. Incidentally, the elder son, Anthony, predeceased his father, so George became the next earl in either 1489 or 1490 (sources differ on the date). I couldn't find whether this family, the Greys of Ruthyn, had any connection to Elizabeth Woodville's first husband, Sir John Grey of Groby. Obviously, the Woodville connection was almost too good to be true from a novelist's point of view and provided the perfect reason for Seb and Emily's return to London, ready for their next adventure.

The church of St Thomas the Apostle in Foxley still has a portrait of Bayard and his wife painted on the gates of the rood screen that they donated to the church. Whether he was steward of the manor, I don't know, but the date of the painting fits and Bayard must have been a man of standing and wealth in the village to be able to afford to be commemorated in this way. There are also the faint remains of the red pigments of a large mural, subject unknown, behind the pulpit on the south wall.

Elsewhere in the village, there are the remains of a medieval moated manor house, but these were fenced off when we visited and all my ideas for its layout were gleaned from old maps.

The Street is still the only named thoroughfare on the eastern side of the main road and extends as far as Foxley Wood Nature

Reserve – all that is left of a vast forest. It is still worth a visit, especially in April and May, for its famous swathes of bluebells.

The idea for the actual murder in the story came from an ancient Chinese tale of the first known solving of a murder by using a forensic technique – in this case, 'flies' and their uncanny ability to detect the smallest specks of blood. However, the implements used in China were the smaller sickles, not scythes.

Special thanks go to John Harvey, Churchwarden at St Thomas's Church, who was a source of great knowledge and a perfect gentleman.

TONI MOUNT

The Seventh
Sebastian Foxley
Medieval
Murder Mystery

THE

COLOUR

OF LIES

The Colour of Lies is due out Late 2018

Join Toni Mount's mailing list and get a
FREE BOOK
PLUS you'll get advance information about future books by Toni Mount...

www.madeglobal.com/authors/toni-mount/download/

Prologue

He had waited a long time for this moment – nigh two years of wandering, homeless and friendless, sneered at for a stranger and suspected as a foreigner. Somehow, he had survived such miserable journeyings. He had hated the German Lands, loathed France and everything about its people but, most especially, he had despised the Low Countries, if for no other reason than that was where he had been abandoned, discarded as of no account. 'Revenge is a dish best served cold,' so they said and, in this case, there was not a vestige of warmth remaining.

There had never been a plan but always an intention. And now he had both a means of avenging the waste of years and making money out of it. God knows, he needed money; sick and tired of being a pauper.

The theft had been as straightforward as any impulsive action could be: a sharp blow from behind to the unguarded head of the unwary watchman, so-called, and the prising open of the locks – at least he had thought to bring an implement for that. Once the door had yielded to his efforts, the wondrous items had been his for the taking. The deed was done, and the matter should have ended there. But now this! Too many accursed foreigners had made his life a torment. All across the northern lands of Europe, merchants, lords and blackguards had vexed him, swindled him, plagued him. And now one more fool – from the Low Countries, as was almost to be expected – would deny him his desire. It could not be. He would not allow it.

The largest of his ill-gotten prizes was as fine a weapon as nature could devise. He raised it high, holding it in both hands like a mace and brought the blunt end crashing down upon the fellow's head. It made a most satisfying sound in the half-light: the crunch of bone and the liquid slap of a brain destroyed. The wretch fell upon his back, bleeding on the withered clumps of grass in the darkness, but it was not enough to appease the sudden flare of anger that overwhelmed him. He reversed the exquisite weapon and plunged the spear-like point into the victim's chest.

It was done. Breathless and weary of a sudden, he withdrew it and wiped its beauty clean of blood. Nothing should mar such a fine and valuable thing. It was worth a king's ransom. Now it was his and, after years of desperation, revenge tasted sweet indeed.

Chapter 1

Tuesday, the eighteenth day of August in the year of Our Lord 1478

London

THE CITY greeted us upon this summer day, sweltering in the heat and enfolding us in its same old stink made worse by our months of absence. I could see poor Adam – a newcomer to the stench of London – nigh gagging upon the unwholesome airs. No doubt but the unaccustomed sultry weather made it more intense. I could not think it healthful for my newborn son either, yet he alone made no complaint of it, sleeping soundly in my wife Emily's arms. Our walk from Norfolk had taken more than six weeks, what with a fortnight passed in Huntingdon after Emily became unwell. I dare say that was my fault, having forced her to travel so soon after birthing our son. It could not be helped, however, since my nemesis, Anthony Woodville, the queen's brother no less, had been about to visit Foxley village, of all places, where I had sought refuge with relatives. Then, during our journey, there were days spent in washing and drying linen for the babe, resting blistered feet and – in my case – a hip joint that caused me to limp by the end of a long day's trudging. The thought that our travels were at an end at last put a smile on my face and I could forgive the city its shortcomings, knowing we were home.

There were five of us, including my dog, Gawain. Myself, Sebastian Foxley, reverting now to the surname I was known by in London. My goodwife with our tiny son, Dickon, who was nigh unto two months in age. And Adam Armitage, my nephew by a much older brother I only discovered recently during our sojourn in Norfolk. Adam be of an age with me and has become more like unto a brother. I was wary of how these two new members of our family would be received, particularly by my true brother, Jude.

To Adam, it was all utterly new. He gaped at the market crowds, the towering buildings, the bustling streets. I wondered what he would have thought of the city's Midsummer Watch – a festival we had missed, unfortunately – and St Bartholomew's Fayre still to come in a week's time, when the crowds would be greater by tenfold. As we entered the city by Bishopsgate, I was able to show him Crosby Place, the mansion that was lately the Duke of Gloucester's London home and Adam's eyes grew wide as cartwheels as he stared at its grand portal, its pinnacled gables and numerous chimneys. Yet the buildings wore a coat of dust that muted its colours, the result of a few weeks without rain, as well as the lack of activity within its walls since Lord Richard had departed for the North Country. All London wore a similar pale shroud in the shimmering haze.

Despite the heat, life went on as usual. The noise of the city was deafening after the quietude of the countryside, and as we pushed through the afternoon crowd in Cornhill, I saw Adam pull his cap down to cover his unaccustomed ears. Apprentices cried their masters' wares, each trying to out-shout his neighbours. Cattle bellowed in the Stocks Market, a gaggle of geese squawked their raucous shrieks of feathered alarm and a laden donkey brayed in protest at the birds swirling about his hooves. Costermongers yelled, iron-rimmed cartwheels clattered over cobbles and goodwives argued for a bargain. These were the sounds of an ordinary day in London, as Adam would discover. Emily saw a group of her friends gathered by the conduit in Cheapside and, of course, they wanted to see the babe and hear all her news, but she waved them away, promising with a weary smile to tell them everything on the morrow.

Thus, we reached our home by St Paul's – its towering spire another reason for Adam to crane his neck and gasp – but if I believed in returning home to London we could resume our life as it was before, how wrong was I? The house and workshop were still standing in Paternoster Row, having neither burned down nor collapsed in disrepair during our enforced absence and I expected some things to have changed since March last. For one, my brother Jude should have wed sweet Rose. But so much was not as I thought it would be.

Our little party arrived hot, tired and travel-stained, entering the familiar yard through the side gate as we always did and making for the kitchen. We were greeted in the kitchen by a squeal of delight from our gap-toothed serving wench, Nessie, who flung herself at me with such enthusiasm that I staggered under her weight which was more considerable than I remembered.

'Master Seb! You're back!' she cried, breathing onions in my face. 'I knew you'd come soon. I told everyone you would. Mistress Em, is that the babe? Let me see.'

'Nessie, I pray you, let us draw breath,' I said.

Emily sat down with a sigh of relief upon a bench by the board and eased the babe into her lap, flexing her arm now released from its burden.

Adam gazed around in wonder at the kitchen which was of a size with the entire cottage we had dwelt in back in Foxley village.

'This place is a palace, Seb,' he said. 'What must you have thought of the dog kennels we call home?'

'I thought they were wholesome and full of kindly welcome.

What more did we need? We were content, Adam. Now, Nessie, pour us all some ale, if you will? And water for Gawain. Where be your manners? This is Adam Armitage. He will be biding with us. Come now! I know he be fine and handsome but cease gawping at him and fetch us drink.'

Adam laughed, seeing her staring and fluttering her eyelashes. He would learn soon enough that Nessie fell in love – aye, and out again – with every pair of breeches that crossed the threshold, be they butchers' apprentices or noble knights. Both had smitten her in the past.

I kicked off my dusty boots, flexing cramped toes, and bade Adam do likewise. After a sip of ale, I knelt and unfastened Emily's shoes for her as she began unwinding the babe's swaddling bands to change his wet tail-clout. I passed her the bundle of linen we had brought with us from Norfolk, though there was little left that remained clean, but that could be put to rights now.

'Where are the others?' I asked Nessie as I put a ladleful of cool water in a bowl for the dog. He lapped it up gratefully.

She shrugged.

'Out.'

'What? All of them? Who be attending to customers in the shop? What of our work?'

She shrugged again.

'Can I hold the babe?' She asked Emily, holding out her arms. This was Nessie's way of avoiding making answer.

I sat on a stool, thankful at last to ease my hip. Warm weather aided it considerably, but we had walked so many miles these last weeks, rest was welcome.

'You may hold him after you answer Master Seb's question,' Emily said, sounding stern as she re-pinned the swaddling bands in place around the babe. Fortunately for us all, he was proving a placid little soul, our Dickon.

'Well, I don't know, do I? Nobody tells me what they're doing; just "do this, Nessie; do that, Nessie; fetch water, sweep the floors, chop the onions, wash the pots". Master Jude goes out first thing, Tom and Jack disappear to the Lord knows where and me and Mistress Rose do all the work. That's all I know. It'll be better now you're back. Is the great hound really Gawain? Ain't he growed so.'

Feeling disquieted by Nessie's words – though how true they might prove was not to be relied upon – I went along the passage to the workshop. Mayhap, I should have been pleased to see it was neat and spotless, not a sheet of paper nor a quill pen nor a pot of ink out of place. However, it did not please me in the least for it was clear that not a stroke of work had been done there all day, perhaps all week. In the shop, the counter board was not lowered, opening on to the street, that prospective customers might see our books and pamphlets for sale. In fact, the door was firmly closed, inviting no one in to browse or buy. The shelves were well stocked and dusted, but I swear the items for sale were the same ones as had sat there back in March when we left London. Had Jude even opened the shop during our time away? I began to have my doubts.

Back in the kitchen, Emily was already inspecting the larder for stuff that might go in the pot for supper. The bacon, onions and peas that had been intended to feed five mouths would now have to stretch to three more, and I was hungry indeed. No doubt, Emily and Adam were also. My wife was grumbling about the lack of provisions.

'There's naught worth having on these shelves but a morsel of cheese and wilting herbs,' she complained.

''Tis otherwise in the shop,' I said. 'The shelves be as full as when we left and with the very same items still for sale. Nessie, has Master Jude sold anything of late?'

'Can't can he? Shop's shut, master.' Nessie blew her nose upon her apron and turned her back to me.

'I can see that, but why?'

'Not allowed,' she muttered.

'What is it that be not allowed? Tell me.'

'Shop's shut 'cos the guild says so. That's all I know.'

'The guild says so? Why would they? This makes no sense to me.'

'With that wretched brother of yours, naught ever makes sense,' Emily said with a heartfelt sigh. 'This is his fault, of course.'

'Now, Em, you must not apportion blame afore we know the facts of the matter. This may have naught to do with Jude.'

'You never should have trusted him to run the business, Seb. It was doomed to go awry.'

'What else was I to do when we had to leave in such haste?' I turned my hands, palms upward: empty.

'I cannot say, but I know who will have to sort out the mess – you! Now you must excuse me. I have a babe to feed.' With that, Emily swept out and retired to the parlour. Like Nessie, she would turn her back on the problem. I wished I could too.

'Not the welcome you would have hoped for, eh, Seb?' Adam said, reaching out to touch my arm in a gesture of reassurance.

'No. Nor the best way for you to come join us. I apologise for the lack of comfort and warmth of greeting for you. This is not how it should be. Nessie, more ale for Adam, if you please?' I watched her refill his cup, spilling droplets on the board, careless as ever, but what was the point in reprimanding her? She would never change. 'When Jude gets home, I be sure he will explain everything. 'Tis all a misunderstanding, no doubt, about the shop.'

'Aye, no doubt,' Adam said, sounding unconvinced, pulling at his close-shorn beard as he often did when thinking. We heard sounds in the yard: a woman's light step and Rose came in, laden with a basket of vegetables.

'God give you good day, Rose,' I said, feeling my heart skip with the same pleasure I had every time I saw her, the greater for months of parting.

'Seb! My dearest, dearest friend.' She set her basket on the floor to embrace me.

I kissed her soft cheek, fragrant and cool as flower petals, and returned her joyous smile.

'How do you fare, lass? You be well?'

'In good health, aye. And you? Where is Emily?'

'Nursing our babe in the parlour: a boy-child. We named him Richard. But I must introduce you both. Adam, this is Rose, my brother's wife. Rose, this is Adam Armitage, my near relation and, by happenstance, a fine scrivener. He will be staying with us and working here until he be settled.' I saw Adam's eyes brighten and his lips part as he took her hand. She affected most men thus.

'I-I must correct the, er, introduction, I fear,' Rose stammered, shaking her head. 'I am wife to no man.' Her voice roughened with unshed tears.

'How so, Rose? What of the wedding? It was all arranged.'

'There was no wedding. Oh, Seb, Seb. It was the worst day of my life.'

How blind and foolish had I been not to notice that she failed to conceal her hair as a goodwife must, nor was there a ring upon her finger.

'Never turned up, did he, that Master Jude,' Nessie said, unasked, as she took parsnips and coleworts from the basket and flung them in a bowl of cold water.

'Oh, I be that sorry, Rose. He seemed so set upon it. Oh, sweet lass, I apologise for his lack of thought. If I may make amends in any way?' I held her close, feeling her tears soaking through my clothes.

'Well, I've never met him,' Adam said, 'But if he turned from taking you to wife, then he must be the greatest fool on God's earth.'

I set a stool for Rose and gave her my ale to drink, that she might be restored somewhat.

'Can you speak of it, lass?' I asked. 'If it doesn't distress you beyond bearing to tell of it?'

She sipped the cup and dried her eyes.

''Tis such a tale of woe as you never heard, Seb. All was ready upon Easter Sunday: the food for the marriage breakfast, my new gown, everyone invited... I was so happy at the thought that next day Jude and I would be man and wife. Then he went to the Panyer Inn with his fellows, as they insisted, to celebrate his last few hours of freedom from the yoke of wedlock. He didn't return. The following morn, we all assembled in the porch at St Paul's: the priest, the guests, everybody. But not Jude. He never came. Eventually, one of his so-called friends arrived, still stinking of drink and piss, his nose bloodied, to tell us Jude was in Ludgate lock-up. There had been a brawl in the tavern and Jude was the cause...' Rose took a shuddering breath.

'My poor lass,' I said, stroking her hair in an act of consolation.

'But that is only half the story and not the worst of it,' she went on. 'You see, the fellow with whom Jude picked the quarrel ended with a broken arm and half-blinded in his eye. Being a scrivener like Jude, such injuries made it impossible for him to work for many weeks and even now he can't see properly, though his arm is mending.'

'Who is he that suffered so?'

'That is the sorriest part of it: 'tis Ralph Clifford, may God aid us.'

'Sweet heaven. Jude could not have done more harm if he had betrayed the king himself.'

'Why?' Adam asked. 'Who is this Ralph Clifford?'

'The son of John Clifford, the Warden Master of the Stationers' Guild.'

'Oh. That's bad indeed.'

'Now Jude is in the good graces of no man,' Rose said. 'Warden Clifford has had him fined and banned from trading for bringing the guild into disrepute; the Dean of St Paul's has fined him for failing to turn up for our wedding, and even the innkeeper at the Panyer has forbidden him to drink there again, since the place was wrecked during the fight. Oh, Seb, you have returned to find us in such straits as I would not wish upon my vilest enemy and never upon my dearest friend. We have all betrayed your trust so dreadfully.'

'No, Rose. Not you. Never say that. This be Jude's doing and no other's. Where is he? Do you know?'

'At his new favoured tavern, I suppose, drowning his sorrows, as usual, having naught else to do these days. He'll be at the Hart's Horn in Giltspur Street, if you know it?'

'Aye, I know it. 'Tis run by a respectable woman, Mistress Fletcher. He'd better behave himself in her tavern for she won't allow any troublemaking under her roof.'

'We see little of him, in truth,' Rose said. 'I think he is too ashamed.'

'Does he sleep here or lodge yet at Dame Ellen's place as before?'

'Dame Ellen has turned him from her door. As I said: he is in no one's favour now. His bed in his old room here sometimes looks to have been slept in but often not. He rarely eats with us, preferring the food at the Hart's Horn, I believe. Now and then I find a heap of his soiled linen in his room and clean shirts disappear from the clothes press, but that appears to be his sole reason for coming home. When he is here, he barely speaks to any of us, spending his time in the parlour, shunning our company to sit alone, brooding and scowling. If I ask how he fares or if he has need of anything, he ignores me. He has never once mentioned the wedding...' Rose drew a long, quivering breath to steady herself. 'I know not where I stand concerning this last, Seb, whether we will ever be wed or no. It seems unlikely.'

I wondered at her words; that she should even want to marry my brother after what had come to pass. She must have read the query in my eyes.

'Aye, I know 'tis utter madness, but I am fond of him still, Seb. He has suffered such misfortune of late, but it was just one moment of foolishness that caused it all. If only it hadn't been

Ralph Clifford he struck.'

'But it was, and now we all suffer the consequences. First thing upon the morrow, I shall go to the guild and see what may be done to restore our business and our reputation, though the damage to both sounds serious indeed. At least I have not offended the guild insofar as I know. Mayhap, I will be permitted to reopen the shop and commence trading once more, though Jude be forbidden. I pray it may be so. But what of Tom and Jack? What have they been about all this while?'

'Little to the good, I fear, and naught to improve our standing. They take no heed of a word I say. Gossip has it that Jack has been seen crossing to Bankside too many times of late. I know not where Tom goes. Perhaps they go together.'

'Bankside be a den of brothels, gambling houses and unlicensed taverns on the far side of London Bridge. Such shady dealings go on there as you would hardly believe,' I explained to Adam who pulled a face but said naught. What was there to say? Matters went from bad to worse. A master was responsible for the good behaviour of his apprentices, and it seemed mine were running wild.

Almost as if the speaking of their names had conjured them from the air – it being nigh suppertime by now – the unruly pair entered the kitchen with a racket that sounded more like a riotous mob than two youngsters. They stopped short at sight of me. They were unkempt and smelled of strong ale and more unwholesome things also.

'M-master Seb. It's you, ain't it?' Jack said, being the first to recover. I noted the faint bloom of manly fluff upon his chin, and I swear he had grown another hand's span since Lent.

'Aye. 'Tis me, Jack, in the very flesh.' I drew myself up as tall as I might: we were much of a height now, but he hung his head and slouched over to a stool. Tom would not meet my eye either. Both lads knew they were disgraced without my speaking of it.

Supper was served, somewhat tardily. We sat at the board as of old but with Adam taking Jude's place. I introduced him to the lads and he spoke briefly of his home in Foxley and why he had come with us to London. Otherwise, little was said at all, and I could not say what we ate. The lads were silent as grave markers. Emily and Rose spoke in whispers to each other, mostly about the babe, with Nessie adding her occasional heedless pennyworth.

For myself, I was, of a sudden, so beset by problems, I felt overwhelmed and unable to voice my tumultuous thoughts coherently. My mind was in such turmoil as to what should be done to begin to mend matters. I ought to speak with Jude afore I did anything but, in truth, I could hardly dare contemplate what I should say to him that would be other than a torrent of curses. Mayhap, it was for the best if we did not meet afore I had calmed myself and done what I might to order my thoughts, aye, and my tongue. But, as with all events this day, the avoidance of just such a meeting proved impossible, for my brother came home as we finished our supper.

Although by no means incapable, he was plainly the worse for drink, belligerent and maudlin by turns.

'What the bloody hell are you doing here?' Was his greeting to me.

''Tis good to see you, Jude,' I said, despite his words. I went to embrace him, but he stepped aside to avoid my gesture of brotherly affection. 'Oh, well, mayhap I should introduce you to our close relation from Foxley village, Ad...'

'Why are you here, Seb? What have you come for? Go back to bloody Norfolk, can't you? I don't need you here.'

'It seems to me that you do need me, Jude,' I contradicted him. 'What in heaven's name have you done to our business, you witless idiot?'

'Sod the business. Is that all you care about? Bloody guild ruined it, not me.'

'But our good name and reputation: what of those?'

'Get off me!' Jude snatched his arm away, and I realised I had been grasping his wrist. He turned on me, teeth bared in a snarl, his fist raised to strike me full in the face. But the blow never landed. Adam was there, twisting Jude's elbow so he cried out that it was breaking. Adam released him but shoved him back onto a bench, and Emily clouted him with her favoured weapon: the broom. For good measure, Gawain seized his boot betwixt his teeth.

'Who the hell are you, you damned bastard? Wrenching my bloody arm like that,' Jude demanded of Adam once things quieted. He was rubbing his arm and wincing. 'And get that bloody mutt out of here.' His booted foot lashed out, but Gawain was sufficiently nimble to avoid it.

'I'm your nephew and all legitimate, upon my honour,' Adam said, grinning and holding out his hand in greeting, though Jude ignored it. 'So pleased to make your acquaintance, dearest uncle!' He burst out laughing. 'You should see your face: a smacked arse never looked so shocked.'

It took the lads a moment or two to understand Adam's words, what with his broad Norfolk way of speaking, but then they were chortling with merriment, and I was hard put not to join them. Jude's scowl was more fearsome than a basilisk's.

'Don't you dare bloody mock me, else I'll knock you into the midst of next month, you miserable dog turd.'

'Miserable? Indeed not, uncle. Dog turds are a nuisance, 'tis true, but the dog always feels better for having made them, and they are greatly appreciated by the tanners' craft. Now, shall we not shake hands and be friends, as well as relatives?' Adam offered his hand a second time.

'Relatives be damned. You can all go to hell!' With which parting shot, my brother stormed out, slamming the door as hard as he could. He was still cursing us from the yard. We heard him even through the thickness of oak, and we sighed with relief, though I was saddened that our reunion had gone so badly. I was none the wiser as to our difficulties with the guild either but no doubt I should learn the worst in the morning.

We retired early: Rose to her lonely bed in the little room she used to share with Kate, my talented young apprentice whom I hoped might return to us soon. Tom and Jack went to their attic and Adam had our old bedchamber at the back of the house – that which should have been Rose's bridal bed with Jude. Emily and I were to occupy the lately refurbished large chamber above the parlour where the glazed window – aye, there were eight glass panes in it – looked out across Paternoster Row to St Paul's. Rose had made a splendid job of cleaning out the mice and spiders that had inhabited the room for so long, making new hangings for the bed and a woven rush mat for the floor. Pride of place though went to the rocking cradle, intricately designed and wonderfully made by Stephen Appleyard, Emily's father, for his first grandchild. It even had a hinged canopy that folded back, so there was no danger of catching the infant's fragile head as he was lifted in and out of the bed. Little Dickon would sleep in princely comfort there.

In truth, I did not expect to sleep at all that night, not only because my mind was a-swirl with the troubles of the day, but because of the noise of the city even after dark. The ringing of church bells, the shouts of the Watch and the constant barking of dogs: these were sounds I had forgotten in the quiet of Foxley village. Yet my exhaustion was such that I slept deeply. Even the midnight wails of the babe failed to disturb my slumbers.

Chapter 2

Wednesday, the nineteenth day of August

The Stationers' Hall in Ave Maria Lane

The Stationers' Hall was not so grand as those belonging to the Goldsmiths' or Mercers' Guilds, but it was, nonetheless, an imposing building, backing on to the Bishop's Palace and facing the ageing but overly ornamented facade of Pembroke Inn across the way. The hall's pale stonework had shed much of its customary lichen cloak, the dry heat of recent weeks having scorched it away. A gull, up from the river, perched on a cornice, fixing me with its evil yellow eye. I made the sign of the cross to bless myself. I needed no additional superstitious fears to weigh upon me; I had burden sufficient as it was. I always admired the gargoyles; one, in particular, reminded me in a kindly way of my old master, Richard Collop, and of habit I usually smiled up at the carving. But not today.

Despite the blazing sunshine, the hour was yet early, and Stationers' Hall was still in shadow. Above the grand entrance, the vivid paintwork of the guild's coat-of-arms – my own handiwork of a twelvemonth since – was dulled to sombre shades. I suppose it suited my downcast humour that it should look so colourless.

The great studded doors might have been Hell's portal, and I dreaded what might await me on the other side.

One half of the door stood open, and I went in, wondering how my fellow stationers should receive me. The perfumes of parchment, paper and hot humanity eddied in the gloom. A knot of men stood just within, all of them known to me.

'I greet you well, good masters,' I said, touching my cap. 'May God grant you blessings this day.' The group parted to make way for me, like the sea before Moses, gowns rustling softly as wind in the trees. 'Good day, Master Benedict,' I said to one. 'How do you fare? I trust your wife and children be well? And Master Jameson, is your mother improved in health since last we met?'

Both men regarded me as if I carried some vile contagion.

'Master Foxley,' Benedict acknowledged brusquely but then turned his back. Jameson ignored me, saying naught but returning to his conversation with the others. I did not speak to the rest for they all moved away, shunning me. I went further into the hall, seeing Warden Clifford standing by the dais, talking with Richard Collop, who had previously held the same office. Since I had worked hard as Master Collop's apprentice not so long since, I was sure that he at least would still prove a friend. As I approached, Warden Clifford saw me. His brow drew down, and his face darkened like an approaching storm.

'So you've returned,' he growled. 'I am surprised that you dare show yourself here.'

'Good day, Warden Clifford; Master Collop. I greet you well. God's blessings be upon you both.'

'We have no business dealings with you Foxleys. You're no longer welcome in this company. Be off with you!' Clifford's anger was blatant as he shook his fist, but Master Collop smiled at me.

'Now, now, John,' he said, laying a hand upon the warden's shoulder. 'The trouble was not of young Sebastian's making.

Don't blame him for the hurt done to your son.'

'I pray that Ralph is mending, sir,' I said to the warden.

'Aye, no doubt you do, but we're still suing that wastrel brother of yours for compensation through the Lord Mayor's Court for the grievous harm he did. We are determined upon it.'

'Oh? I know naught of that, Master Clifford. In truth, I have exchanged so few words with Jude since my return yesterday, I be here to discover what came to pass precisely and to enquire as to when I may reopen my shop.'

'Never, if I have anything to do with it. You Foxleys are a disgrace to the guild.'

'That's not fair, John,' Master Collop said. 'Sebastian is a highly respected and industrious member of our fellowship.'

'They're folios cut from the same inferior parchment: each as bad as the other.'

''Twas not Sebastian who brought the stationers into disrepute. And remember,' Master Collop added in a whisper which perhaps I was not meant to hear, 'The Duke of Gloucester is his patron. We wouldn't want to offend the king's beloved brother, would we?' He winked at me, and I smiled in return. Richard Collop was indeed still my friend; God be thanked.

About one hour later, I returned home with a more spritely step and a somewhat lighter heart. With ill-grace and grudgingly, Warden Clifford had permitted me to open the shop and trade once again, though it would require the approval of a full meeting of the guild to reinstate the name 'Foxley' in the memoranda rolls from which it had been struck out – a revelation which had shocked me indeed. At length, he had heeded the wise counsel of Master Collop, however reluctantly, admitting I was not at fault in the matter. Thus, I had good tidings to impart – with one unfortunate proviso for the resumption of business: Jude was not to be a part of it. This distressed me, but mayhap it would not bother my brother so much?

I entered through the front door, rather than by means of the side gate, calling out:

'Tom! Jack! Come. Let down the shutter-board straightway. We be open for trade, directly. Hasten, everyone. 'Tis business as usual.'

At least Rose answered me, hurrying into the shop.

'You mended matters with the guild, then? I knew they would listen to you, Seb,' she said as we lowered the shutter onto its trestles to form the shop counter. She began arranging a few of the best books upon it, hoping to entice customers, polishing the covers with her apron so they appeared bright as possible.

'Aye, after a fashion, at least.'

'Is there still a difficulty?'

'Our name is not yet reinstated. That will take a while, I fear. A-and... well, Jude is forbidden to be my partner. How long he may be barred from the trade, I know not, but there it stands. That be the situation for now.'

Rose nodded but said naught. I suppose, like me, she wondered if Jude would care.

Adam appeared in the doorway.

'So it's back to work, after all, Seb?' he said with a grin. 'You'd best show me what's to be done if I'm to earn my bed and board.'

'I shall be delighted to do so, shortly, but where are those two scallywags? I told them to await my return, did I not?' I strode along the passage to the kitchen. Emily was suckling the babe at her breast. Nessie was scrubbing the board clean. But of Tom and Jack, there was no sign.

'You had success with the guild, I hear?' Emily said, lifting little Dickon onto her shoulder and patting his back to wind him. 'That's a relief. Our funds from Lord Richard are all but spent. We need money, husband, and swiftly.'

'I be aware of that, Em, but a master also needs his apprentices. Where are they?'

'After breaking their fast – which you have yet to do – they went out to the yard. Tom said he would see Gawain did his business out there and Jack claimed his boots needed cleaning. I should have been suspicious of Jack cleaning anything, but I had Dickon to see to. Neither of them has come back since. They must have gone slinking off like a pair of miscreants as soon as your back was turned. They need a good thrashing with my broom, and they'll get it when next I see them, the idle young scoundrels.'

Emily was right: I had not had breakfast, so I helped myself to ale.

'Is there bread and cheese, Nessie?' I asked.

She shoved a platter at me, all ungraciously.

'And don't go dropping crumbs on that board what I just scrubbed.' So much for respecting her master.

There came a scratching at the kitchen door. It was the dog but not the lad who was supposed to be with him. No one else was in the yard. I let Gawain in and shared my cheese with him.

In the workshop, Adam was already making use of his knowledge of our craft, preparing a batch of quills. He had soaked them in water and was now heating sand over a small brazier before plunging the ends of the feather shafts into the sand to harden them. The day was already hot, and such a task was an uncomfortable one. Sweat stood out on Adam's brow, and his tunic looked damp beneath his arms.

'We'll also need ink before we do any work,' he said, wiping his forehead on his shirt sleeve. 'What was left has dried up. Do you buy it ready-made or make your own?'

'I prefer to make it up to my own receipt, especially for any high-quality work but, since that takes time and we have no prestigious commissions outstanding, I suppose I'll have to purchase some for the present. Jack can fetch it from St Paul's.'

'From the cathedral across the way?'

'Aye. There are stationers who have their stalls in the nave.'

'Then let me go. I should like the chance to see inside the place. Besides, your Jack's not here, and I'd be glad of a breath of fresh air after this.' Adam set the last quill to cool and fanned his flushed face with a rag before using it to wipe grains of sand from his hands.

'That would be a kindness, Adam,' I said, giving him a couple of coins from my purse. 'But enquire first who the Pullen brothers may be.'

'You want I buy from them?'

'Far from it. Avoid them, Adam. Their ink be so inferior, I wouldn't trust it to write a list for marketing, for fear the words would fade afore I got there. And a toothless old fellow by the name of Giles Honeywell: his wares be of a good standard but, if you purchase anything from him, don't mention that you work with me.'

'Oh? And why not?'

'Because my previous journeyman, Gabriel Widowson, upset him mightily one time by destroying the relics that he was also licensed to sell. Giles has never quite forgiven me, despite my recompensing him for his losses. Dean Wynterbourne wasn't much pleased either.'

'Then 'tis as well your new journeyman knows how to behave himself in church,' Adam said with a laugh. I heard him chuckling with Rose as he went out through the shop. I was glad that someone could bring a little merriment into the Foxley household. Ink might be in short supply, but good humour was a greater lack.

It was many months since I had last sat at my desk, but it felt good to be back in my right and proper place. My pigment brushes were like old friends well met, and I was eager to use them again. With no work requiring my attention, I decided it was time I renewed my acquaintance with my drawing board, so I took up my old leather scrip to confirm its contents. There was my small board, my supply of charcoal and both red and white chalks. There was paper also, including the sketches I had done of the Duke of Clarence – may God assoil him – preparatory to painting his portrait. I wondered if it would ever be painted now; whether Lord Richard would write to me with instructions concerning it. All was in order otherwise except for the scrip itself. I remembered the stitching of the shoulder strap had worn to a few threads and required mending. Afore we departed London in haste, I had meant to re-stitch it. I doubted it would last another outing otherwise, but it was a task I could do now.

'Sewing? Is that a task for you, husband?' Emily came into the workshop, cradling little Dickon in the crook of one arm, a dish of savoury pastries in her other hand. She set down the dish upon my desk and stood watching my efforts with needle and linen thread. 'Here. You take the babe, and I'll have that stitched in no time,' she offered.

It was as well: my handiwork with a needle was not of the best and probably wouldn't last a week. I gave up my stool to her and took Dickon in my arms. I had got used to holding him now, but it had taken a while to lose my fear of dropping him. I was pleased to see that he was awake, his blue eyes – so like his Mam's – gazing up at me. A shaft of morning sunlight through the window caught his wispy halo of hair, turning it to gold thread against the drab cloth of my old doublet. He gurgled and blew a bubble of spit. It seemed he was laughing at me. Aye, a doting Papa be a fine jest indeed.

I began to sing to him, taking him back to the kitchen and out into our little garden across the yard. The pig greeted us with a contented grunt, wallowing in the patch of mud Nessie had created in the sty to keep her cool. Dickon blew bubbles at her too and waved his arms eagerly. Then I showed him the small hard apples ripening on our solitary tree. The tall stalks of fennel rattled their seed heads in the hint of a breeze. I picked a stem and held it for him. He seemed fascinated by the noise it made when shaken but then grabbed at it, dispersing most of the seed so it made the pleasing sound no longer. He yawned, showing his moist, rosy tongue. I sang him a lullaby, and he was quickly asleep, but I liked the soft weight of him in my arms and was in no hurry to put him in his woven basket back in the kitchen.

A cluster of sparrows chirruped and quarrelled on the roof of the pigsty, looking ragged as beggars in their moulting feathers – a reminder that summer was past her prime. Others might complain of the heat, but I dreaded the onset of autumn's chills and with them the return of pain in my hip. It was a penance I paid every winter, so I determined to make the most of the warm season.

Back in the workshop, Emily had repaired my scrip with her perfect stitchery and was eating one of the pastries.

'Try one, Seb: cheese and thyme. See what you think.'

I handed the babe to her.

'His nether end has been making some ripe noises,' I warned her. 'And I detect a definite fresh stink.'

She laughed.

'And you did not dare investigate further, I know.'

'That be a mother's privilege.' I helped myself and took a bite of one of the savouries.

'Poor little Dickon. What he would have to suffer if it were left to his Papa to tend to his tail-clouts. Come, my sweeting. Let Mam clean you up.'

'These pastries be delicious, Em,' I called after her as she left the workshop.

After dinner – for which meal my errant apprentices had miraculously reappeared – I determined to walk to Smithfield to watch the preparations for St Bartholomew's Fayre that would begin on the following Monday and go on for the rest of the week. I should take my drawing stuff, certain there would be plenty of subject matter in all the hustle and bustle that preceded the annual event of the largest cloth fayre in England. But a less pleasant task must take precedence: the rebuke of Tom and Jack. The application of discipline was never a skill of mine but, on this occasion, it was required. Not wishing to be heard in the shop for fear of deterring any customer, I took the pair out to the yard.

They stood before me. Tom frowned down at his shoes, kicking the dust. Jack eyed me with an air of defiance, but at least he looked me in the face.

'Explain yourselves. As soon as I went from the door this morn, you two scuttled off, not to be seen again until mealtime. There was work to be done, yet you absconded.'

'Abs-wot?' Jack said, out of habit, ever querying my choice of words. I was in no mood to enlighten him.

'Where were you? Tom. You give me answer first.' I stood, arms folded, waiting. My anger was simmering. 'Tell me!'

''Cross the bridge,' he muttered without looking up.

'To Bankside?'

He nodded.

'Why? What business have you there?'

'None.' He shrugged.

'Jack? Were you there also?'

'Wot of it, if I wos? No law 'gainst it, is there?'

'You wretched pair. Naught which occurs in Bankside can possibly be of any credit to our good reputation.'

'Wot reputation? Master Jude's dragged it in the shit long ago. We ain't got no good reputation no more, so wot's it matter wot I do?'

'It matters more now than ever, Jack. We must restore it.'

Jack snorted, and I came so close to clipping his ear – closer than I ever had afore.

'If you fink we need a beatin', you should start wiv yer bruvver. Worse than us he is, ain't he?'

'Are you telling me that Master Jude visits Bankside?'

'The Cockpit, the Cardinal's 'At, the Blue Dolfin. He's been t'all of 'em. We've seen him, ain't we, Tom?'

Jack had just named the most notorious gambling den, the most infamous brothel and the tavern that was the most vicious nest of crime in Southwark. If he spoke truly, then reprimanding the lads would serve little purpose when my brother was the one destroying our good name so utterly, I feared it might be beyond saving.

'Get about your work, both of you. Tom, start the preparation of ink, then rule up pages for a half dozen cheap primers. You know how well enough. Jack, you can whiten parchment for a fine book I have in mind to begin. Think you can do that without covering the workshop in chalk dust?'

'Wot for? We ain't allowed t'sell nuffink. Guild says so, don't it?'

'No longer. We be in business once more, as of this morn. I persuaded Warden Clifford to permit us to open the shop again. There is a stipulation, however, that need not concern you at present.'

'A stipilashon? Is that a good fing, then?'

'Any more shirking of your tasks or sneaking over to Bankside and I'll not be so lenient next time. Understand?'

'Aye, Master Seb,' they replied in unison. I wondered if they meant it, sighing at the urgent need to reclaim some measure of respect for the Foxley name. It would not be easily accomplished, especially if Jude was intent upon tarnishing it yet further. We would have to speak on this matter, but I dreaded confronting my brother concerning his misdeeds.

With Emily having taken little Dickon with her to collect some silkwork from Dame Ellen in Cheapside, I could not improve my humour by playing with my son. So to cheer myself, I left Tom and Jack in the workshop, under Adam's watchful eye, and went in search of inspiration for my next book – an illustrated version of Aesop's Fables. Folk of all ages enjoyed those short, moral tales but I had it in mind to include marginalia of amusing figures – human bodies with animal heads, each appropriate for the story – thinking it would appeal to children as they learned to read. I suppose I envisaged little Dickon chuckling over the images when he was older and smiled at the thought. Already, I was in better humour.

When I arrived with Gawain at my heel, Smithfield was humming like a beehive, men erecting canvas tents, wooden booths and setting up trestles for their stalls. Packs of merchandise and innumerable baskets and barrels of wares for sale were stacked everywhere, some in precarious piles that looked about to topple. It was a scene of colourful chaos and so much noise. Men shouted, packhorses whinnied, donkeys brayed, and dogs yapped. Canvas awnings cracked and flapped as they were unfolded, wooden supports were hammered home into the sun-hardened ground, and laden barrows groaned and creaked as they trundled over the scorched grass. Of a sudden, a small barrel fell from a leaning stack, its lid coming loose, spilling the contents across the ground. The scent of cloves on the breeze identified the strewn spice, and a foreign tongue cursed it.

I sketched whatever took my eye while doing my utmost not to hinder the work in preparation for the fayre. We had a close call when a large dog took a sudden dislike to Gawain and charged at us, growling like a demon, jaws drooling. Fortunately, he was tied to a post, left to guard his master's wares, which duty he accomplished admirably. The rope pulled him up short afore he could sink his fearsome teeth into my leg or Gawain's. Poor Gawain dared not stray an inch from my side after that encounter and his tail drooped for some while as it rarely did.

Returning with a sheaf of sketches and a wealth of inspiration for my Aesop's Fables, I was greeted with a smile from Emily as I entered the kitchen.

'Such news, Seb,' she said even afore I had set down my scrip. 'Dame Ellen has arranged for a stall at the fayre, that we might sell our silken stuffs and Rose may sell the gloves she has been making in our absence. Is that not a most excellent opportunity to get us recognised among the finest mercers and drapers?'

'Aye, indeed it is.' I poured myself some ale. I was parched on such a day. I filled Gawain's bowl with water, certain he must be dry also. 'Do you have much to sell?'

'Well, not as much as I might have hoped, though there is the orphrey I finished just before we left London and some other few pieces of gold threadwork. I could do naught in the way of silkwork while we were in Norfolk, now could I? But Dame Ellen's other outworkers have been busy, and with Rose's gloves there will be plenty to sell. We will all take turns to serve at the stall. I am so excited, Seb.'

'I be glad for you, Em,' I said, taking her in my arms and kissing her lips.

'None of that, husband.' She pushed me aside. 'I have ribbons and girdles unfinished that could be ready in time for the fayre, if I work on them every minute I may. Here: you take Dickon for a half hour, and I can set up my weaving frame in the parlour afore suppertime.' She put the babe in my arms. 'He's been fed and his tail-clout changed. You can manage him, can you not?'

'Aye, I suppose...'

'Nessie. Get that coney skinned and jointed and put it in the pot for supper and watch that cherry pie doesn't scorch while you keep it warm on the hearthstone, you hear?'

'Aye, Mistress Em,' the maid gave me a look of resignation as we both were directed in our tasks.

With Emily busy in the parlour, I took Dickon and my scrip through to the workshop. I was both pleased – and somewhat surprised – to find a scene of industry. Adam was copying out a text, Tom was ruling pages, and Jack was decanting ink from a pig's bladder into small stoppered pots, ready for use. This last was the most unusual in that he had spilt not a drop. He had also made a decent effort with four sheets of perfectly whitened parchment without shrouding the workshop in chalk dust.

'I see you have done a good afternoon's work. I commend your diligence. Thank you.' I put my scrip on my desk and hooked the stool with my foot, pulling it out so I might sit with the babe upon my lap.

'We are in your employ. You feed us and give us a roof over our heads. In return, we work.' Adam looked up with an expression of puzzlement. 'Is that not how it's supposed to be, Seb?'

'Aye, it is. But that has not always been the case of late. Has it?' I fixed first Tom and then Jack with my eye.

Tom muttered something under his breath that I could not make out.

'We had no reason t' work when Master Jude got us shut down, did we?' Jack said, stoppering the last ink pot. 'Weren't no point us doin' fings wot would never get sold, was there?'

'Your logic is impeccable,' I said, 'But things have changed now.'

'Im-wot-able?'

'Faultless, Jack. And we have our reputation to restore.'

'Aye, 'til Master Jude picks anuvver fight wiv anuvver important fat arse 'ole.'

'Jack! I will not tolerate such speech. You will say extra prayers this eve to cleanse your mouth. Five Aves and two Paternosters at the very least.' It was fortunate my little son was deep asleep; I would not have him hear such words at so tender an age.

'Sorry, master.'

'Adam,' I said, turning to a more pleasurable subject. 'What did you think of our cathedral? Fine, is it not?'

'It took my breath away, Seb, in every way.' Adam set down his pen. 'The stained glass is a wonder indeed and far more bedazzling than the cathedral in Norwich. And the nave is so vast. The fellow from whom I bought the ink told me it's the longest nave in all of Christendom. Is that true?'

'Maybe.'

'But what robbed me of my breath was the stink of it. So many sweating bodies were hardly the worst of it. I expected that, but you never warned me about the cheese sellers, Seb.

Their wares were that ripe they could stun a fellow at fifty clothyards distance, I swear.'

'I had forgotten about that. In hot weather, the goodwives are permitted to sell their butter and cheeses in the cool of the nave, else you'd need a bucket to carry home your purchases. The butter would be melted and rancid and the soft cheeses gone runny. It has always been the way of it every summer.'

'And such a din as all the sellers shouted out to get my attention. It seemed amiss to me in the House of God – so much yelling and distraction.'

'You must attend vespers there one evening. The choristers make a more heavenly sound. And, thinking on it, I ought to pay my respects to the precentor, letting him know I be available once more, if he requires my services.' I picked up a quill, untrimmed as yet, and tickled 'neath Dickon's dimpled chin, setting him gurgling with pleasure.

'You sing? I mean, I know you can; I've heard you in Foxley church and at your work. But you sing in St Paul's?'

'It has been known,' I said, feeling heat rise in my cheeks. I wished I hadn't mentioned it. I lifted the babe to my shoulder to conceal my reddened face from Adam.

'Master Seb's got the best set o' lungs in London, ain't he?' Jack said, adding to my discomfiture. 'Sang fer the bishop last Christmastide, he did.'

At that moment, little Dickon stirred in my arms. Perhaps he was too hot in so many layers of swaddling and held close against me. I realised my chest was damp with sweat – his and mine.

'Dickon needs some fresh air,' I said. 'I shall be in the garden if you need me.' Thus, I escaped from the embarrassing discussion.

Jude had returned, seemingly in a more mellow humour since he had spoken with civility to Adam and taken time to acknowledge little Dickon. After supper, he and I were alone in the kitchen. Everyone else had retired, including Adam who still kept countryman's hours and was frugal with candles. I had spread my sketches made earlier across the board, to choose the most suitable for the Fables but I was only postponing the matter I dreaded. The moment had come when I could delay my conversation with my brother no longer, concerning his actions during my months of enforced absence. I poured more ale for both of us, certain we should need it. Jude took the cup and drank deep even as I braced myself to commence the speech I had been rehearsing in my head. How to reprimand my brother without having him fly into a temper?

'Jude. We must talk about...'

He held up his hands, stilling my words of reproach afore I began.

'I have to tell you: I'm going, Seb,' he said, though he still sat at the board.

'To the Hart's Horn, I suppose? Give my regards to Mistress Fletcher, but first you must hear what I have to say.'

'No. You don't have to say anything. I mean I'm leaving, leaving London.'

'What? But why? Why would you leave now, when we've hardly been reunited since I returned from Norfolk?'

'You've seen something of the world beyond London. Now it's my turn.'

'But that was not from choice, and I need you, Jude. I cannot manage without you.'

'You most surely can, as your months away have proved. You don't need me anymore, little brother. Besides, you've got Adam to help in the workshop now.'

'Of course I need you still! Adam is not my brother.'

'He might as well be. You two are grown close.'

'If you be jealous of him, there is no need...'

'Seb, listen to me. You have a wife, a child, a business to run.

You're a good man. You work hard, and folk respect you. You've made a success of your life. Whereas I've made a bloody mess of mine from one end to the other.' He sighed with the weight of his words. 'This is my chance to begin anew; make a fresh start.'

'But, Jude...'

'You'll not persuade me otherwise, so save your breath. The others will be glad to see me gone.'

I gulped my ale; my hands a-tremble with the shock. Mayhap, that was partly true. Emily would be relieved and, most probably, the lads would not mind if he left, dreading his punishments as they did.

'Rose will not be glad at all,' I blurted out. 'She loves you, Jude.'

He laughed, but there was no humour in it.

'She should count her blessings that the wedding never took place, else she'd be shackled to me forever and forced to come with me.' He reached across the board and ran a melancholy finger along the bones in my hand, one by one. 'She'd hate that, seeing 'tis you she truly loves. She only said she'd wed me to be close to you. Well, now she's free of me. I shall not hold her to any promise.'

'You speak so much nonsense, Jude. None of that be the truth in the least.'

He pushed back from the board and regarded me for a long, thoughtful moment, then shook his head.

'Of course it is. 'Tis all too true: Rose loves you, little brother; not me. You must be blind if you see it not. Anyhow, I'll be gone first thing.'

'Where will you go? What will you do for money? How will you earn your bread? How long will you be away?'

'Don't concern yourself. I haven't yet determined where I'll go.'

'Huntingdon is not so far and looked to be a goodly town when we were there a little while...'

'France, maybe?'

'No! Not there... across the Narrow Sea. To England's enemy?'

'Perhaps Bruges, then. An Englishman will get a friendlier welcome in Burgundian lands, no doubt. Or Rome?'

'I do not see you as a pilgrim, Jude. You cannot go...'

'Did I mention a pilgrimage? No. 'Tis just a city I'd like to see.'

'What about money?'

'A scrivener can earn a few pence anywhere, reading or writing letters for others.'

'In French or Dutch?'

Jude shrugged.

'Latin will serve me well enough, particularly in Rome, if I go there. I have no worries about money.'

'When do you intend to leave?'

'As I told you: first thing in the morn.'

'So soon? Oh, Jude, not yet. It is too sudden. I need to prepare myself.'

'For what? I'm leaving; not you. Besides, you left London without a word.'

'There were men attempting to kill me, as you well know. I wanted to bid you farewell, but Lord Richard's good sense prevailed: the streets were too dangerous for me then. If-if you be certain of your intent, I shall come with you as far as...'

'No, Seb. I want no miserable, long farewell. I shall be gone by first light. Have a good life, little brother.'

Of a sudden, I felt empty inside, as though I had been hollowed out. I stared at him, memorising his face to the last blemish, every bristle on his stubbled chin but, mostly, his eyes. Would I remember them: the deepest shade of lapis lazuli, if I never saw him again?

'Jude, please. I cannot bear to...' Tears leaked and ran down my cheeks. I grasped his arm as if to save myself from drowning. 'Please. I beg you. I love you, Jude.'

'Enough! Don't try to talk me out of this. My mind is set upon it.' He pulled himself free of me. 'Don't make such a bloody fuss. You're a man, not some wet-eyed, lovelorn wench.'

I nodded and wiped my face with my palms. I made a

pretence at tidying the sketches but selecting the most suitable for the Fables book was of no importance any longer. My brother was leaving: I could scarce believe it. I sipped the last of my ale. Without looking at him, not wanting to burden him with my boundless sorrow, I touched his hand softly, having his warm flesh against mine. It was reassuring to feel his strength one last time.

'You are right. We both have to live as we think best. May God be with you always, Jude, my beloved brother. There will ever be a welcome for you here when your purse runs dry, which it undoubtedly will.'

Without another word, Jude nodded at me and left the kitchen to seek his bed. Long after, 'til the candle burnt down, I sat with my faithful Gawain, his head resting against my knee. I think the creature knew and understood my distress, my sense of loss, gazing up at me with dark eyes brimful of sympathy, his wet nose nuzzling my fingers. It felt like a bereavement to have Jude go from me of a sudden, and it hurt like a blade piercing my heart. But if such was his decision, who was I to speak against it? It was his life to be lived as he saw fit. I would pray God to keep him safe and guide him on the righteous path, yet I doubted that was the way matters would betide. Jude was never one to take the straight road if there looked to be an intriguing diversion. God had granted mankind self-will, and my brother ever took full advantage of it.

Toni Mount, a member of the Crime Writers' Association, earned her Masters Degree in 2009 by researching a medieval medical manuscript held at the Wellcome Library in London. She enjoys independent academic study and has also completed a Diploma in Literature and Creative Writing, a Diploma in European Humanities and a First Class Honours Degree from the Open University.

Toni has written several well-respected non-fiction books, concentrating on the ordinary lives of people of the Middle-Ages, which allow her to create accurate, atmospheric settings and realistic characters for her medieval murder mysteries. Her first career was as a scientist, which enhances her knowledge and brings an extra dimension to her novels. Toni writes regularly for both The Richard III Society and The Tudor Society and is a major contributor to MedievalCourses.com. She is a qualified teacher and regularly speaks on a variety of topics at venues throughout the UK.

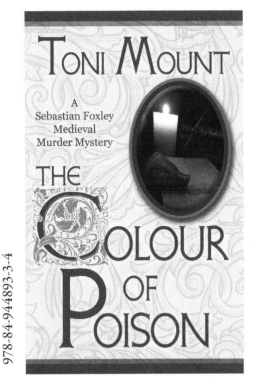

Toni Mount

A
Sebastian Foxley
Medieval
Murder Mystery

The Colour of Poison

**The first Sebastian Foxley
Medieval Mystery by Toni Mount.**

The narrow, stinking streets of medieval London can sometimes be a dark place. Burglary, arson, kidnapping and murder are every-day events. The streets even echo with rumours of the mysterious art of alchemy being used to make gold for the King.

Join Seb, a talented but crippled artist, as he is drawn into a web of lies to save his handsome brother from the hangman's rope. Will he find an inner strength in these, the darkest of times, or will events outside his control overwhelm him?

Only one thing is certain - if Seb can't save his brother, nobody can.

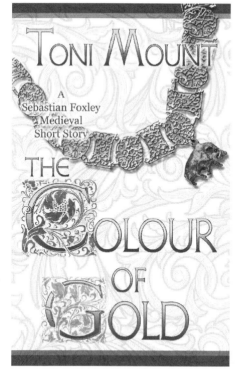

978-84-946498-0-6

The second Sebastian Foxley
Medieval Mystery by Toni Mount.
A short story

A wedding in medieval London should be a splendid occasion, especially when a royal guest will be attending the nuptial feast. Yet for the bridegroom, the talented young artist, Sebastian Foxley, his marriage day begins with disaster when the valuable gold livery collar he should wear has gone missing. From the lowliest street urchin to the highest nobility, who could be the thief? Can Seb wed his sweetheart, Emily Appleyard, and save the day despite that young rascal, Jack Tabor, and his dog causing chaos?

Join in the fun at a medieval marriage in this short story that links the first two Sebastian Foxley medieval murder mysteries: *The Colour of Poison* and the full-length novel *The Colour of Cold Blood.*.

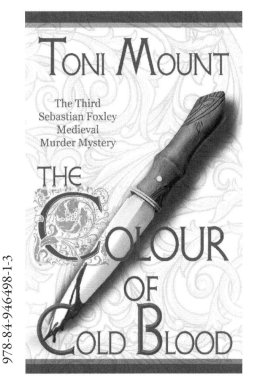

TONI MOUNT

The Third
Sebastian Foxley
Medieval
Murder Mystery

THE COLOUR OF COLD BLOOD

978-84-946498-1-3

**The third Sebastian Foxley
Medieval Mystery by Toni Mount.**

A devilish miasma of murder and heresy lurks in the winter streets of medieval London - someone is slaying women of the night. For Seb Foxley and his brother, Jude, evil and the threat of death come close to home when Gabriel, their well-liked journeyman, is arrested as a heretic and condemned to be burned at the stake.

Amid a tangle of betrayal and deception, Seb tries to uncover the murderer before more women die – will he also defy the church and devise a plan to save Gabriel?

These are dangerous times for the young artist and those he holds dear. Treachery is everywhere, even at his own fireside…

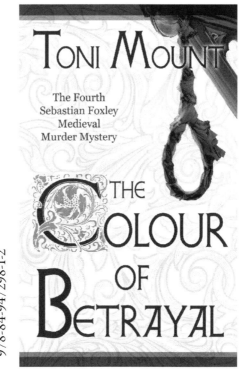

TONI MOUNT

The Fourth
Sebastian Foxley
Medieval
Murder Mystery

THE

COLOUR

OF

BETRAYAL

978-84-947298-1-2

**The fourth Sebastian Foxley
Medieval Mystery by Toni Mount.
A short story**

Suicide or murder?

As medieval Londoners joyously prepare for the Christmas celebrations, goldsmith Lawrence Ducket is involved in a street brawl. Fearful that his opponent is dying from his injuries, Lawrence seeks sanctuary in a church nearby.

When Ducket is found hanging from the rafters, people assume it's suicide. Yet, Sebastian Foxley is unconvinced. Why is his young apprentice, Jack Tabor, so terrified that he takes to his bed?

Amidst feasting and merriment, Seb is determined to solve the mystery of his friend's death and to ease Jack's fears.

978-84-946498-0-6

TONI MOUNT

The Fifth
Sebastian Foxley
Medieval
Murder Mystery

THE COLOUR OF MURDER

**The fifth Sebastian Foxley
Medieval Mystery by Toni Mount.**

London is not safe for princes or commoners.

In February 1478, a wealthy merchant is killed by an intruder and a royal duke dies at the Tower. Neither case is quite as simple as it seems.

Seb Foxley, an intrepid young artist, finds himself in the darkest of places, fleeing for his life. With foul deeds afoot at the king's court, his wife Emily pregnant and his brother Jude's hope of marrying Rose thwarted, can Seb unearth the secrets which others would prefer to keep hidden?

Join Seb and Jude, their lives in jeopardy in the dangerous streets of the city, as they struggle to solve crimes and keep their business flourishing.

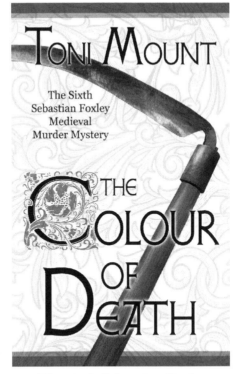

978-84-948539-1-3

**The sixth Sebastian Foxley
Medieval Mystery by Toni Mount.
A short story**

Seb Foxley and his wife, Emily, have been forced to flee medieval London to escape their enemies. They find a safe haven in the isolated Norfolk village where Seb was born. Yet this idyllic rural setting has its own murderous secrets and a terrible crime requires our hero to play the sleuth once more.

Even away from London, Seb and Emily are not as safe as they believe - their enemies are closer than they know and danger lurks at every twist and turn.

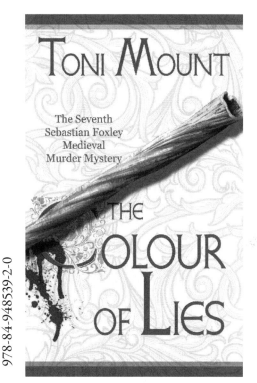

978-84-948539-2-0

**The seventh Sebastian Foxley
Medieval Mystery by Toni Mount.**

It is late summer and London is all a-bustle for
St Bartholomew's Fayre, with merchants arriving from faraway
lands. When an old friend returns with fabulous items for sale,
it can only mean one thing: trouble. As thievery, revenge and
murder stalk the fayre, Sebastian Foxley – artist and sometime-
sleuth – has mysteries to solve. In uncovering the answers, he
becomes enmeshed in a web of lies and falsehoods. His greatest
dilemma means having to choose between upholding honour
and justice or saving those dearest to him. How can a truly
honest citizen of London practise deceit and yet live with
his conscience?

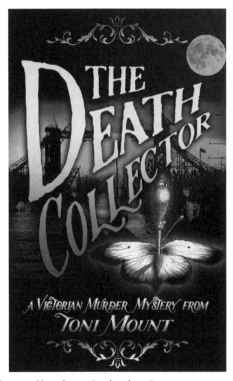

978-84-948539-4-4

More dastardly than Jack the Ripper; more vile than a London Particular, an arch-fiend prowls the Victorian city streets. Nobody is safe from his experiments, whether peer or prostitute, preacher or policeman in this murderous melodrama. Will Inspector Albert Sutton, aided by his wife Nell and her cat, be able to unmask and apprehend the heartless killer, or will they become the next novelty specimens of the Death Collector?

In this riveting novella, Toni Mount explores the darker side of Victorian London, creating a gripping thriller packed with shocking murders, unexpected twists and chilling suspense.

Read it if you dare ...

Get your FREE BOOK!

https://www.madeglobal.com/authors/toni-mount/download/

Historical Fiction

The Sebastian Foxley Murder Mysteries - **Toni Mount**
The Death Collector - **Toni Mount**
Falling Pomegranate Seeds - **Wendy J. Dunn**
Struck With the Dart of Love - **Sandra Vasoli**
Truth Endures - **Sandra Vasoli**
Cor Rotto - **Adrienne Dillard**
The Raven's Widow - **Adrienne Dillard**
The Claimant - **Simon Anderson**

Non Fiction History

Anne Boleyn's Letter from the Tower - **Sandra Vasoli**
The Turbulent Crown - **Roland Hui**
Jasper Tudor - **Debra Bayani**
Tudor Places of Great Britain - **Claire Ridgway**
Illustrated Kings and Queens of England - **Claire Ridgway**
A History of the English Monarchy - **Gareth Russell**
The Fall of Anne Boleyn - **Claire Ridgway**
George Boleyn: Tudor Poet, Courtier & Diplomat - **Ridgway & Cherry**
The Anne Boleyn Collection - **Claire Ridgway**
The Anne Boleyn Collection II - **Claire Ridgway**
Two Gentleman Poets at the Court of Henry VIII - **Edmond Bapst**

PLEASE LEAVE A REVIEW

If you enjoyed this book, *please* leave a review at the book seller where you purchased it. There is no better way to thank the author and it really does make a huge difference!
Thank you in advance.

Printed in Great Britain
by Amazon